根

以讀者爲其根本

莖

用生活來做支撐

引發思考或功用

獲取效益或趣味

安德魯+陳俊郎◎著

◆孩子學英文的路上，總是挫折不斷、成效不彰？

◆如何為孩子佈置、準備一個隨時隨地都可以接觸到英語的學習環境？

◆有誰能夠幫幫這些家長及孩子？

18年美語教學經驗名師安德魯&孩子王俊郎哥哥

教學心法、不傳密招全公開!! 讓你學好英文不花冤枉錢

前言

在本書的最開頭，我們想以為你們禱告的方式開始！

是的，沒錯！當我們現在正著手寫這一本書時，我們也同時在為您禱告。

一、如果您是父母：

我們禱告上帝會賜給您充足的智慧，所以經由這一本書的幫助，您可以花最少的時間和金錢找到最適合您孩子的英文課程。

二、如果您是英文老師：

我們禱告這一本書可以幫助您再一次的檢視自己的教學方式和目的，以成為一位更有效率的老師，並幫助您的學生把這一個目前世界上最重要的語言學得更好。

三、如果您是英文補習班負責人：

我們禱告這一本書可以幫助您評估自己的英文課程，所以您可以分辨教材和教學方法的好壞，進而創造一個更建全的英文課程。

Preface

Let me begin by saying this: We are praying for you. Yes, that's right, even now as we are writing this book we are praying for you.

If you are a parent

We are praying that God will bless you with wisdom, that this book will help you to save both time and money as you seek to obtain the best English education for your child.

If you are an English teacher

We are praying this book will help you to examine your methods and purposes in teaching, that you will become a more effective teacher and guide your students to a better command of this most important language.

If you are an English school administrator

We are praying this book will help you analyze your English programs, that it will help you differentiate between good and bad materials and methods, and then help you create more effective programs.

一般人學習英文時常犯的錯誤

把學英文當成一場牌局

很多人把學英文當成是在賭場玩牌。他們在不同的牌桌徘徊，當找到一個看似有趣的牌局，他們坐下來玩幾把。如果贏了，他們會再繼續玩；如果輸了，他們可能移到另一桌去玩，或者續繼留在同一桌玩下去，希望可以把輸掉的贏回來！

學英文不是一場牌局

把學英文當成解九連環

有另外一些人把學英文當成是只有天才才解得開的九連環。從第一步開始，咬緊牙根、埋頭苦幹，盼望著哪一天可以解開每一個環節。但心裡卻有這樣一個聲音說道：「從以前到現在，真正完成這個艱鉅任務的人似乎不多，而且也不知道這漫漫長路何時才會結束！」終於，這樣子的想法讓他們一再的半途而廢。

學英文不是解九連環

選擇英文補習班不該碰運氣！

還有另外一票人——這些人在亞洲很常見；他們對英文學習一竅不通，所以他們為自己的小孩選擇英文補習班的過程往往都存著碰運氣的心態！結果呢？可想而知，小孩的學習效果往往不如預期。他們的孩子很多在英文補習班打轉了好幾年，可是卻沒真正學到多少東西。

The Card Game

Many people approach English language learning as a casino card game. They look around at different gambling tables, choose one that looks interesting to them, sit down and play a few rounds. If they win, they keep playing for a while. If they lose, they either move onto the next table or continue playing in the hope that they'll eventually win it back.

* **English is not a card game.**

The Puzzle

Other people approach English as some horrible puzzle that only geniuses can solve. Start at square one, grit your teeth, sweat, work and work until you finally finish the puzzle, though few people ever do and who knows when it will ever end? Hmm, just thinking about that discourages me from ever trying.

* **English is not a puzzle.**

The Blind Darts Game

Then there's a group, quite common in Asia, who feel they haven't the slightest clue as how to learn English, so when they decide where to send their kids, it's like putting on a blindfold and throwing a dart at a board. Result? They rarely hit the board. Kids go to special "English" schools for years and hardly learn anything.

* **English is not a darts game.**

學英文不可以碰運氣？

那英文是什麼呢？

一、 英文是一個語言；一個活生生、不斷改變、演進、美麗又有力量的語言。

二、 只要方法對了，每一個人都可以學好英文的。

三、 學英文是一種時間和金錢的投資；這和其他的投資一樣都需要經過精心的規劃才能真正從中獲利。

本書最主要的目的在於幫助您如何投資時間和金錢在英文學習上，同時提供指引讓您可以替孩子找到最合適的英文學習管道。如果孩子們可以學好英文，他們將擁有悠遊在這個資訊爆炸時代中的能力。此外，他們會比別人有更多的機會，因為他們可以和這個世界的許多人溝通！

最後，我們謹獻上我們最真誠的祝福，希望您和您的孩子在學習英文的路上一路順利！

Andrew Rent 陳玲郡

So what is English?

1. English IS a language, a living, moving, evolving, beautiful and powerful language.

2. English CAN be learned by almost anyone.

3. It IS a major investment of time and money and should be treated as any other investment - with respect. Take the time to research the investment. Will it most likely produce a profit or a loss?

This book is lovingly written to help you make the wisest investment of your time and money. We hope this book will help you to find the best teachers and programs to help your child learn English well, in order that your child will be able to navigate in this increasingly small and complex world, and be able to take full advantage of all the wonderful opportunities which are out there - to people who are able to communicate in English.

We send our blessings to you and wish you and your children the best in mastering this wonderful language.

Sincerely,

目 錄

Book outline

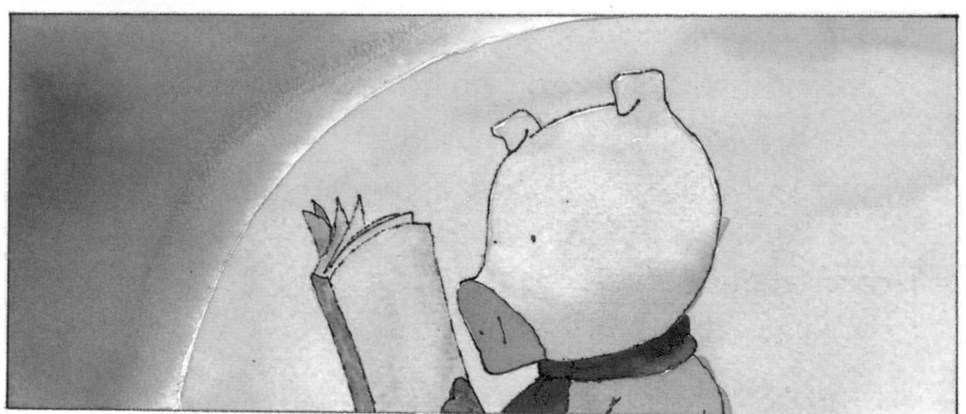

英語學習的介紹

Introduction to English language learning

英文學習所涵蓋的範圍很廣，幸運的是，無論是想要學好英文的人，或是想幫孩子找到理想英文學習環境的家長，都不需要對英文學習有太深入的了解和認識。

然而，如果能對相關的概念有一些認識，學習英文(或是任何一種語言)時都會有某些程度上的幫助。

英文教科書的選擇

首先要避免坊間許多兒童英文教材常犯的錯誤。過去我們用過許多不同種類的英文教科書；有些教科書只偏重於閱讀技巧，有些則強調口語能力的訓練卻忽略了讀、寫和翻譯的練習。甚至有一些英文教材是所謂的「圖畫書」－－也就是強調用圖畫來介紹單字。但這種教材卻往往沒有教學生如何將所學到的單字串連成句子，學生也就無法將所學的內容用在真實情境的溝通。當然每一種教科書都有其優點，但是我個人覺得這樣子的教材不適合當做英文學習時的主要教材來使用，因為如果以語言學習該涵蓋的眾多層面而言，這些教材有其不足的地方。

因此，英文教科書的選用應該注意到學生聽、說、讀、寫各能力的平衡。對母語非英文的國家而言，學生學了英文之後往往很少有機會可以練習他們所學到的東西。基於這個原因，如果語言學習只著重在學生口語的訓練是很不實際的，其理由如下：一、因為學生很少有機會練習所學到的東西，他們很快就會忘記學過的東西。二、以一個非英語系國家而言，不論是學童或成人，學習英文時最常接觸到的往往是以書面方式呈式的英文。因此，閱讀這個重要的技巧不可以被忽略。除此之外，閱讀能力的提昇可以進一步的增強口語能力。這樣一來，學童不但可以學得更快，還可以更快速、更正確的吸收單字和句型概念。

The subject of English language learning and teaching is huge. Fortunately, there is no need for a person wanting to learn English or a parent wishing to find a good teacher or school to research this subject in depth.

However, there are some basic ideas and methods anyone wishing to learn English (or most any other language) could benefit from by gaining a cursory understanding.

Choosing an English Textbook

Avoid the pitfalls of so many children's English textbooks. In the past, we have used some books that emphasize reading to the exclusion of other skills, while others go the opposite direction and focus on verbal skills while avoiding reading, writing, and translation. Still others are "picture books," with the emphasis on pictures introducing vocabulary items without any system for tying the words together in coherent sentences building up to true communication. While each method has its advantages, we feel that such books, if used as a core curriculum, lack crucial aspects of total language acquisition.

Instead, look for a more balanced approach. The fact of English language learning in most international settings (where the native language is not English) is one where children rarely have an opportunity to use the English they are learning. As a result, focusing exclusively on verbal skills is usually impractical for two reasons: 1. Children will have little opportunity to practice, and so will quickly lose/forget the skills. 2. Living in non-native English environments, whether as children or adults, they will most often come in contact with the written word, so this fundamental skill should not be ignored. In addition, combining reading with verbal skills reinforces both, allowing children to learn faster and enabling them to more accurately absorb both vocabulary and concepts.

記憶力和注意力

準備好要來學一些專有名詞了嗎？我想你大概不太喜歡。然而，請儘量保持清醒，因為如果可以理解以下的這些概念並將他們有效的利用，無論是你本身或是你的小孩在英文學習上都可以更上一層樓的。

「記憶」大概可分為以下三種：短期記憶(STM)、長期記憶(LTM)及永久記憶(PM)。短期記憶，顧名思義，指的是一種很短期的記憶－－記憶的時間大約只有20～30秒而已。當我們聽到一些東西時，如果沒有去覆述它，經過20～30秒之後我們就會把它遺忘了。像我太太請我幫她買衛生紙，如果她沒有再提醒我或我沒有在心中覆誦幾次，這件事可能很快就會被忘記了。現在應該就知道為什麼去購物中心時常常忘了要買什麼了吧！

下一個概念是長期記憶；長期記憶的記憶時間大概可以維持到幾個小時，甚至幾天。如果我出門時對自己說：「好，我一定要記得買衛生紙回家。」在進購物中心時我又對自己說了一次。可想而知，這一次我一定會記得了。這就是長期記憶的部份。然而如何讓長期記憶變成永久記憶呢？那就要看學習者專注的程度了，這也就是以下所要談的－－頻率和強度。

頻率

「分散式」和「集中式」的學習有很大的差別。以下是一個分散式學習的例子：如果你想給學生十個單位的學習量，將這十個單位分散開來學習會比一次給學生十個單位來得有效。舉例來說：可不可能在三十分鐘內讓學生學會「星期幾」的英文單字呢？大多數人可能會回答：「當然沒問題」，然後花整整三十分鐘讓學生不斷的重覆講這七個單字(而這對大人和小孩來說通常是很無聊的)。然而得到的學習成果往往如下：學生的確在30分鐘內記

Notes on Memory and Attention

Are you ready for some specialist terms? No? Well, try to stay awake. If you can learn some of these key concepts and then apply them effectively, you can greatly boost your own or your child's learning.

Are you aware that there are different kinds of memory? There is a difference between short-term memory (STM), long-term memory (LTM) and permanent memory (PM). Our STM for what we hear is very short--perhaps only 20 or 30 seconds. This is how long something we have just heard will remain available without it being repeated. My wife tells me to buy some toilet paper. If I don't hear that again, by her or by me saying it to myself in my mind, then it'll probably be gone in a minute. Now you know why you forget to buy things at the supermarket, right? The next step up is LTM, which may last a few hours or even days. "Okay, I've got to buy that toilet paper," I say to myself as I walk out the door, and then again to myself as I go into the store. See? Now I remembered it, this time. To then move information from LTM to PM depends largely on how well the learner's mind is engaged--a matter of frequency and intensity.

Frequency

There is a very important difference between distributed and massed practice. Here's an example of distributed practice: if you give a student ten exposures to some item but these exposures are interrupted by exposure to other items, the student is more likely to retain that item than if the exposures were all given in one bunch. For example, let's say you want your child to learn the English names for the seven days of the week. Can you do that in 30 minutes? Sure, most people would say, and then plunk down to 30 minutes of steady

下「星期幾」的英文單字，可是一個禮拜後，大多數的學生可能都已經忘光了，或者頂多記得其中二個至三個的單字。

那我的做法為何呢？在第一次上課時我會花5分鐘教學生講Sunday(星期日), Monday(星期一), Tuesday(星期二)這三個字，第二次上課復習前三個字，然後再加上Thursday(星期四)。接下來的幾堂課重覆這樣子的做法，我敢保證學生會記得這些單字很久。差別在哪裡？

在第一組中：30分鐘一次做完 → 共花了30分鐘 → 短期記憶

在第二組中：一次花5分鐘分6次做完 → 共花了30分鐘 → 長期記憶

二組學生都分別花了30分鐘在學習同樣的教材上，然而最終得到的結果卻大大的不同；這也就是分散式學習所代表的涵義。長久以來，我們都建議學生，如果一周只有60分鐘來學習英文，分成6天每天花10分鐘練習會比一次花一個小時學習來的效果好上許多(這也就是為什麼我鼓勵我的學生，想學好英文，一天花20到30分鐘來學習的原因)。

強度

就強度而言，可分成以下四個方面來談：

1、**是否生動活潑：**如學生記住彩色圖片的時間會比黑白圖片來得長。

2、**對學生是否重要：**如果學生知道現在上課的內容會在考試中出現，他會更努力的來記住這些內容。

3、**情感層面：**國、高中女學生可能會比國小男童更容易從愛情小說上學到單字。

4、**學習是否可以和學生的想法產生連結：**學生學"chocolate"(巧克力)這個字會比學"indefinite"(不明確)這個字來得快，因為學生馬上可以連結" chocolate"這個概念。

drilling practice (which is usually really boring for both kids and adults). For most students, the result will be this: they'll be able to produce Monday-Sunday in a somewhat efficient manner. Wait seven days, ask them to tell you the days of the week, and most of them will have forgotten, or at best, will remember two or three days.

What would I do? I'd teach them Monday thru Wednesday for about 5 minutes, then the next day, spend 5 minutes in review and add on Thursday. Repeat this for the next few days, and I can guarantee most students will remember the days of the week for quite some time. What's the difference?

Group A: 30 minutes at one time = short term memorization

Group B: 5 minutes a day for 6 days = 30 minutes = long term memorization

Each student spent 30 minutes working on the target material, but the results for one group will be vastly different from the results for the other. That's the idea behind distributed practice. For many years now the authors have been advising students that, if one had only 60 minutes a week to learn English, it would be much better to practice 10 minutes every day rather one hour once a week. (I actually try to convince students to practice 20 to 30 minutes a day for effective language acquisition.)

Intensity

There are four aspects in regard to intensity:

a. **vividness** -- color pictures are remembered longer than black and white

b. **long-term importance to the student** -- if a student knows THIS ITEM WILL BE ON THE TEST, then he'll try much harder to remember it

c. **emotional depth** -- teenage girls will probably learn vocabulary in a love story much faster than elementary school boys

因此，我們想建議老師們(還有關心孩子學習的家長)想辦法讓上課變成更有趣、更刺激和充滿變化的，同時分散學習的時間，多做分散式的練習。

學單字時，單字卡是一項很好的工具，一張單字卡只寫上一個單字。學生每天看著單字卡練習，每天儘可能的多練習幾次，同時有機會的話把這些單字用在真實的情境當中。學生自己製作單字卡和把單字用在真實情境中都可以增加學習的強度，而每天練習則是在頻率上的強化。

注意力

學生學習的效果和上課是否專心息息相關。也就是說，學生如果無法專注在學習的事物上，他們就無法學得很好。英文有一句諺語可以很貼切的形容這種情形：The lights are on but nobody's home.(燈亮著，可是沒有人在家)。如果學生沒有把注意力放在課堂上，學生雖然人坐在教室裡，沒有打瞌睡，可是他的心已經神遊去了，也許想著在某個地方玩、打電動玩具、和女朋友約會或是看電影。不論是哪一種情形，學生等於人不在課堂上，因為他沒有專注的上課，老師所講的東西自然就像是耳邊風了。

因此，家長和老師應注意學生的專注程度。學生是否專注在課堂上？

當然，如果教學是充滿想像力、互動良好、變化多且有趣的，自然就可以激起並延長學生的學習興趣。

老師們應該時常思考下面這個問題：學生上課是專注在老師和上課內容上或者是專注在還剩多少時間上？學生是常常看錶，還是根本就忘了剩多少時間下課？身為老師，我們最喜歡聽到學生說：「什麼？怎麼這麼快就下課了？」當每個學生都專注在課堂上時，時間往往會過得特別快！

d. breadth of associations an item finds in the student's mind -- a student will learn the word chocolate much faster than the word indefinite because he immediately relates chocolate to something he knows and enjoys

Therefore, the authors suggest that teachers (and parents involved in educating their children) work toward making English learning as intense as possible by making it enjoyable, exciting and varied, and that words and structures being learned be divided over time, increasing the long-term frequency.

A simple example for memorizing new vocabulary -- have the student make vocabulary cards, with only one word per card. Have the student practice with the cards every day, more than once a day being optimum, and try to use the vocabulary in actual life situations. If the student writes the cards himself, this increases intensity, as does use in actual situations, and daily practice helps with frequency.

Attention

The quantity of learning will largely depend on the quality of attention students give to it. In other words, if students aren't focused on what is being taught, they're not going to learn. English has a good idiom that applies here: the lights are on but nobody's home. In this case, the student is sitting there in class, he's awake, his eyes are open, but his mind is off swimming in a lake, or playing a video game, or on a date with his girlfriend, or watching a movie. In any case, he's not there. He's not focusing. Whatever the teacher is saying is going in one ear and out the other.

So parents and teachers must be aware of the student's level of participation. Is the student paying attention? Is his mind engaged?

Of course, teaching which is imaginative, active, resourceful, and playfully humorous will help to arouse and sustain students' interest.

不同的語言學習模式

我們大多數人常有一個錯誤的觀念，那就是認為每個人都應該一樣：「小明會這個字，既然大民和他在同一班，為什麼他沒有辦法學會這個字呢？」事實上，每個人的學習模式不見得一樣，每個學生的優缺點當然也會有所差異。有些學生可能發音學得特別好，有些學生則可能閱讀部份學得比較好。我深信每個學生都有把另一種語言學好的潛力，但某些學生在某領域的學習可能就要比別人花更多的時間。使用多樣性的活動可以讓每個學生都有表現的機會，讓他們可以有「發光」的機會！

謹慎規劃的課程

成功的課程往往把重點放在充份地熟練某些特定的字彙或文法概念上。身為一個家長，如果到一家美語補習班去詢問他們某個級數所學習的字彙為何，而這機構的老師或者是行政人員都沒有辦法很詳細的回答這個問題時，那你就知道他們的課程並沒有謹慎的規劃。這就好像說，你到銀行去問你的戶頭裡還剩多少錢，如果得到的答案是：「你戶頭裡是有一些錢，至於詳細數目的話，我們並不是很確定！」遇到這種情形，我想你不可能會再把你的錢放在這個銀行了！

不要忘記：學語言是大筆金錢和時間的投資，放聰明一點！

從一開始學習，學生就應該在一個互動良好的上課環境下學習常用的英文，而且難度需不斷的提高。一個良好的課程包括日常生活用得到的實用會話，至於字彙和句型則會被放到閱讀中。而彩色插圖的使用可以讓一本參考

A simple question to regularly ask: are students concentrating on the teacher and the subject matter, on the class and materials, or on the clock? Are they glancing frequently at their watches, or have they lost track of time? As teachers, we love to hear students say, "What? Is class already over?" Time has flown by because everyone was fully involved.

Different Language-learning Styles

One problem with many of us is that we think everyone should be the same. "Tommy knows how to say that word. Frank's in the same class. Why can't he say that word, too?" There are many different language-learning styles, and students have widely different strengths. One child may be very gifted in learning correct pronunciation, while another may pick up reading almost like it's his native language. I believe that most people can learn another language very well, but it may take a little longer for some people in certain areas. Using a variety of activities gives different students opportunities to "shine" in different ways.

Carefully Controlled Programs

The most successful programs tend to focus on learning English through mastery of carefully controlled vocabulary and grammar. If you, as a parent, go to a school and ask what vocabulary level a certain class is at, and neither the administrator nor the teacher can give you a good answer, then that program is obviously not carefully controlled. Let's say you went to your bank and asked, "How much money is in my account?" If the answer you received were, "Well, you've got some money. How much? Umm, we're not quite sure." I'm guessing

書更出色。更現代化一點的參考書則會安排額外的練習，並利用歌曲、韻文、受歡迎的兒歌，或者甚至是饒口令來增加不同的文化刺激。有許多很好的課程會以一些動作教學－－來就是俗稱的TPR(全肢體回應)－－來做開場。另外，買教科書時，選擇有教導基本寫作和文法概念的教科書(但當然不是強調，尤其是對兒童美語教材而言)。

如果要讓學生真正喜歡上閱讀，讀英文故事書會是一個很好的方法。如果學生以前已經聽過這個故事了，現在再用英文來讀這個故事時學生會更感興趣。舉例來說，如果學生已經學過「三隻小豬」這個故事，現在再來讀英文版的三隻小豬對學生來說就不會太困難，且學生會很有成就感。當然如果故事搭配CD和卡帶就更好了，因為這樣一來可以同時訓練學生的閱讀和聽力。但要特別注意一點，這些故事是否用學生可以接受的字彙程度所寫成的。

何謂「控制字彙」呢？我有看過很多不適合學生使用的美語教材，雖然它們看起來好像都不錯，有彩色插圖，也號稱有限制字彙的數量。然而其單字難度呢？在入門的英文學習書籍中，不應該出現像cheetah, breed和pigsty這一些字。可是我曾看過這一類的單字在所謂的"基礎兒童美語"教材中出現。

在任何語言中，某些特定的字彙會比其他字彙更常被使用。研究發現，在英文中，有100個單字就佔了所有青少年讀本內容的一半！舉例來說，像boy(男孩)、dog(狗)、和girl(女孩)這些字都是所有語言中最常被使用的字。因此，學生應該先學會這些字。不論是學母語或是外語，學童如果可以以一個愉快的方法學會這些最常用的字彙時，他們學習語言的速度會增快許多。因此，當選擇教材或課程時，選擇把學習重點放在學習最常用字彙的教材或課程，因為這樣可以幫助學生很快學會一些最實用和最常被使用到的單

you'd close that account real fast and go looking for another bank.

Never forget: language learning is usually an investment of significant money and a lot of time. Act wisely.

From the start, students should be challenged to learn and use common English in interactive settings that gradually become more difficult. Excellent programs may include useful phrases for daily conversations. Vocabulary and sentence structures are often focused in the readings. Good language books are usually enlivened by colorful illustrations. Modern textbooks often allow for extra practice and some cultural exposure in the form of songs, chants and popular nursery rhymes or even amusing tongue twisters. Many fine programs begin with some teaching of movement and actions, what is known as TPR (Total Physical Response). Also, look for some teaching (but not emphasis, especially for young children) of writing and basic grammar concepts.

For students to build an interest in reading, real enjoyment is often found in storybooks. This may especially be true if a child is already familiar with the stories in his native language. For example, if a child already knows the story "The 3 Little Pigs," then learning how to read it in English can give a sense of accomplishment while not presenting too great a challenge. If the storybook has an accompanying CD or tape, all the better! That will develop both reading and listening. Just be sure that the storybooks are written at an appropriate vocabulary level.

What is superior controlled vocabulary? I have seen some terrible children's textbooks. They may look nice, with good illustrations, and what appears to be a limited vocabulary. But what is the choice in word difficulty? In an entry-level book, words like cheetah, breed and pigsty are not recommended, but these are all words I've seen in "beginning children's English" books. Wow!

字。新單字的比例要被控制在一個學生可以接受的程度，但又要有一定的挑戰性。最後，新的字彙需要重覆的出現許多次，這樣學生才可以徹底的學會這些字的用法並牢記這些單字。

優良的英文教材會把不同的英文能力以不同章節、不同形式表現出來。舉例來說，會話單元中教授的單字可能會在歌曲、聽力、寫作活動和其他活動中再被使用出來。因為不斷的把字彙用在不同的章節裡，新的句型會不斷的被增強而很快的被學會。

老師和家長要特別注意所謂真正語言的學習。語言學習時常犯的一個錯誤我們在這裡把它稱之為「Frere Jacques」效應。我記得在小時候我學一些當時流行的兒歌像「Frere Jacques」(見本節最後)，但是一直到多年以後我學進階法語時才真正了解這首歌的涵義。換句話說，許多人可能都會唱一些英文歌，可是卻不知道這些歌的真正意思為何。對兒童來說，模仿聲音是很容易的，但是真正了解並使用這些單字又是另外一回事了。

由上可知，老師教的不見得是學生所能學到的，而這也就是強調會話式教學一個很重要的缺點，而閱讀/翻譯方剛好可以彌補這一個缺點。簡而言之，老師應隨時檢驗學生是否真正的了解上課內容的意思。

In all languages, certain words are used much more often than others. Research indicates that in English, about one hundred words form about half the total number of words found in juvenile reading. For example, boy, dog and girl are among the most frequently used words in any language. Therefore, these should be taught first. Whether learning a mother tongue or a foreign language, children can accelerate language acquisition if the most common words in a language are learned first and in an enjoyable way. So our advice for new learners is to find materials and/or programs that focus on the most common English words, thereby helping children to quickly learn the vocabulary which will be most useful and with which they will most often come into contact. The rate of introduction of vocabulary should also be controlled to maintain a level at which most students can accept, while remaining challenging. Finally, new vocabulary should be repeated often to aid in memory and help gain mastery.

The best books and language programs integrate the various skills of English by writing them into each lesson as interrelated aspects. For example, vocabulary introduced in a conversation lesson will then be used in a reading, and may be used in different forms in the songs, listening, writing activities, and so on. By constantly integrating vocabulary between different sections of a book, new terms will be regularly reinforced and thereby rapidly acquired.

Both teachers and parents should be careful to monitor actual language learning. One pitfall of language teaching is what the authors term the "Frere Jacques effect." I remember in childhood learning the popular children's song "Frere Jacques" (see below), but not learning the actual meaning of the words until many years later when taking high school French. In other words, we could all sing the song, but we didn't know what it meant! It is easy for many children to simply mimic sounds; it is quite another thing to be able to understand and use those words.

英文為第二外語的教學方法簡介

溝通式教學法：

強調語言學習應該注重想法和感覺的溝通，而這些溝通對學生而言必須有其意義。

聽說教學法：

教學重點放在聲音和句法規則上。

功能式教學法：

強調如何在適當的內容中使用合適的表達方式。

閱讀／翻譯教學法：

語言以書面方式呈現以達到字彙強化的目的。另外，在雙語的環境下，以讓學生翻譯的方式確定他們真正的理解。

肢體反應教學法：

透過動作和語言的關係來強化語言的記憶。

文法／結構教學法：

以文法和結構方式來教學。

Therefore, it is good to remember that what is taught is not always what is learned. This is one disadvantage of over-reliance on conversation methods. The Reading/Translation Approach helps rectify this problem. Simply stated, teachers should regularly check students' actual understanding.

Various ESL Learning Approaches:

Communicative Approach

Learning should focus on communicating thoughts and feelings that are meaningful to the students.

Audio lingual Approach

Focusing on sounds and syntax.

Functional Approach

Emphasizing how to use expressions in their proper context.

Reading/Translation Approach

Utilizing the visual forms of language for rapid vocabulary retention and, in bilingual settings, checking actual understanding through translating bi-directionally from one language to the other.

Total Physical Response

Linking physical action with language to increase retention.

Grammar/Structural Approach

Examining grammar, and using grammar and structural forms to teach the basic forms of a language.

Frere Jacques

法文	中文
Frere Jacques, Frere Jacques	你睡了嗎？你睡了嗎？
Dormez vous? Dormez vous?	約翰, 約翰?
Sonnes les matines, sonnes les matines,	鬧鐘已經響了.
	鬧鐘已經響了.
Din, din ,don. Din din, don.	叮叮咚,叮叮咚

Frere Jacques

法文

Frere Jacques, Frere Jacques
Dormez vous? Dormez vous?
Sonnes les matines, sonnes les matines,
Din, din ,don. Din din, don.

英文

Are you sleeping, are you sleeping?
Brother John, Brother John?
Morning bells are ringing, morning bells are ringing.
Ding Ding Dong, Ding Ding Dong.

設定目標

Setting Goals

目標－－不可或缺的因素

過去這幾年，很多學生和父母到我的補習班說他們想學英文。我總是會問他們這一個問題：「你學英文的目的是什麼？」

然而大多數的學生和家長總是不知如何回答這個問題；或者我應該說，他們似乎從來沒有想過這一個問題。他們只知道學英文很重要，但卻沒有明確的目標。

就成人而言，學英語的目標大概可粗分成以下幾大項：

一、 旅遊英文

二、 商業英文

三、 訓練英文聽力

四、 會話

五、 文法

六、 旅館英文(或者是不同工作場合需要的英文)

七、 閱讀

八、 寫作

...等等不同的目的。

對學生而言，設定目標似乎容易的多了。對大多數學生而言，學英文的意思就是從字母開始學。然而，明確的目標還是需要被設定。設定英文學習目標時可以由以下這幾個方向來思考：

一、 學習的重點是放在會話能力上嗎(口語表達能力和聽力)？

二、 學習的重點是要兼顧英文每個方面的學習嗎(聽、說、讀、寫和文法)？

Goals - a Necessity

Over the years, many students and parents have come to me wanting to learn English. One of the first questions I ask is, "What is your goal?"

I usually get a blank look. A clear goal has never been considered; just the general idea of "learning English."

For adults, here's a simple breakdown:

A. Travel English

B. Business English

C. Listening

D. Conversation

E. Grammar

F. Hotel English (or other professions and industries)

G. Reading

H. Writing

... and the list goes on.

For children, it's usually a little easier. For most kids, it means starting at ABC and working up from there. Still, goals have to be set. Parents and children should consider the following:

A. Will the focus be on conversation (speaking and listening)?

B. Will the focus be on a full language approach (speaking, listening, reading, writing, with grammar)?

C. What is the time frame? Study for 1 year or 6 years?

D. What level of competency is sought?

三、 準備花多少時間學英文？一年？三年？五年？十年？

四、 想達到的目的為何？

1、 擁有基本的英文會話能力？

2、 通過國內某個英文考試(如全民英檢)？

3、 通過國外某個英文考試(如托福)？

另外，以下的學習方式也必需被考慮進去：

1、 一個禮拜要花多少小時？二個小時？四個小時？或者是更多呢？

2、 想找怎樣的老師來上？全部由外國老師來上？全部由中籍的英文老師來上？或者是外國老師和中籍英文老師一起上呢？

3、 以家教的方式(如一對一或少數人共請一位老師到家裡上課)或者是到英文補習班去上呢？

總而言之，在學英文之前一定要有一個很明確的目標。如果沒有設立目標，那又怎能知道自己學習的狀況如何呢？沒有目標的學習就好像是開車上路可是卻不知道自己要開到何處去一樣。

在聖經上有很多充滿智慧的話語，以下是其中一句和目標有關的經文：

「沒有來自上帝的指引，人民就會放蕩無羈」箴言29章18節

這裡有一些有趣的數據：如果隨機取樣一百個年輕人，每一個人一定都有一套自己的成功目標。然而，當他們65歲時再追縱他們的成就時會發現，這一百個人當中富有者只有1人；另外5人過著金錢不虞匱乏的生活；而其他的94人則終其一生都需依賴別人生活。

難道這94人本來計劃要過一個失敗的生活嗎？當然不是！唯一的差別在於這94人沒有好好的規劃自己的人生。

同樣的，這樣子的概念也可被應用在英文學習上(或者可以進一步的說

a. Hold a basic conversation with a foreigner?

b. Pass a national English exam (like the GEPT in Taiwan)?

c. Pass an international exam (TOEFL)?

And the following approaches:

a. 2 hours a week, or 3, 4, 5, or more?

b. All foreign teachers? Or just local teachers? Or a combination of the two?

c. Hire a private tutor (for 1-on-1 or small group) or go to an English school?

I cannot stress enough how important it is to have a clear goal in mind. If you don't have a goal, what do you plan to accomplish? It's like getting in a car, driving out on the road, but having nowhere to go!

There is a great deal of wisdom to be found in the Bible, and here's one verse that relates to goals:

"WHERE THERE IS NO VISION, THE PEOPLE PERISH." PROVERBS 29:18

Here's an interesting statistic. Take your average group of young people. Ask 100 of them what they're doing to guarantee success in their future, then track them until they're 65. Statistically the result will be: 1 will be wealthy; 5 will be financially secure; 94 will live and die as dependents.

Did those 94 plan to fail?

No, they just failed to plan.

The same truth applies to learning English (or succeeding at just about anything). Unless we:

a. have a vision for our future;

b. line up our priorities accordingly;

c. set high standards for ourselves;

d. keep our goals before us at all times

——the probability is we will end up being one of the 94.

是在做任何事上)。除非我們：

一、 對未來有一個好的願景。

二、 依事情的輕重緩急訂定先後順序。

三、 為自己設立高標準。

四、 讓自己無時無刻都有追尋的目標。

不然我們最後的結果可能會成為那94個失敗者其中一位！

設立可達到的目標和時間表是決對必要的，因為如此一來我們才能知道已完成多少及還有多少需要完成。目標必須是可以被檢視的！為什麼大多數的工作要求員工上下班時打卡？為什麼他們有特定的企劃案和時間表？原因在於如果一件事無法被檢視，這一件事就無法被管理。

除非你已確切知道目標在哪裡，否則你永遠也無法達到那個境界。

千萬不要當94個失敗者的其中一位。目標設定的目的在於激勵自己成長，如果一個目標設定之後無法達到這個目的，那這個目標就變成了一個不確實際的想法。設定一個目標時一定要了解以下兩點：

一、 我現在的立足點在哪裡？

二、 我要往哪個方向推進？預定花多少的時間完成？

所以，每一個有心想學好英文的人都該問自己上列這兩個問題。我現在的英文程度為何？我想提昇自己的英文程度到哪一個階段？我要花多少的時間來完成這些目標？

實際一點！

有一次我和小女兒去看一場俄羅斯的芭蕾舞表演，當時她轉頭對我說她想要和台上的舞者跳得一樣棒。我說：「很好！但那要花很多的時間和精力

Achievable goals and deadlines are necessary if we are to know how far we've come and how far we have to go. Goals are measurable. Why do you think most businesses require workers to clock in and out at certain times? Why do they have specific projects and deadlines? If it can't be measured then it can't be managed.

Unless you determine where you're going, you'll never get there.

Don't be one of those 94!

Goals should demand growth, otherwise, they're just a formula for the status quo. A person setting a real goal will clearly understand two things:

A. Where I am now.

B. Where I want to be, and when.

So those are the first questions for any student of English (or parent) to ask.

Where am I now? How much English do I already know? Where do I want to be? How much English do I want to learn? How long will it take me to get there?

 Be Realistic

My young daughter and I were watching a Russian ballet performance. She turned to me and said she wanted to dance like I them. said, "Fine. It takes time and a lot of work to learn to dance that way. When do you want to be that good?"

She answered, "Next month."

Well, it's nice to have high hopes.

I like to use this comparison to help students and parents understand the work involved. How long would you expect to learn piano in order to play well?

練習才能達到那樣的境界，妳打算什麼時候和台上的舞者跳得一樣好？」

「下個月！」我的女兒回答我。

對自己有很高的目標和不切實際差別很大，不是嗎？

我喜歡用以下的比喻來告訴父母和學生，學習英文過程所需付出的努力。學習鋼琴的人要學多久才能彈得好呢？所有的鋼琴老師和演奏家可能都會有同樣的答案：「要持續好幾年每天不斷的練習！」而一些傑出的鋼琴演奏家甚至會告訴你說，一直到現在，他們的學習和努力從未停止過。學習語言不也是一樣嗎？事實上，我深信學習一種語言比學習任何一種樂器都要複雜的許多！

這裡的重點在於，不要指望一個禮拜只去上兩次英文課，練習也不夠盡心盡力，在六個月之後就可以說一口流利的英文！

那，何謂實際的目標呢？

對於一般的小學生來說，如果能一天學會1到2個英文單字，那就很不得了了！很多人也許會不同意我的看法，「一天1到2個英文字？那根本學不到什麼東西嘛！」相信我，這做起來沒有那麼容易。當然，對於某些資質特別好、或對語言有特別興趣的學生來說，這樣子的目標不會太難達成。但是，就我各人的經驗而言，大多數學生無法在一周內學10個英文字(平均一天1.5個字)。如果有辦法照著這個速度來學習，學生在一年當中就可以學500個字了。

這裡特別要提出的是，這裡所說的「學會」並不是指「快速記憶」。我知道很多學生可以為了小考在10分鐘內背完10個單字，但也許隔天再問他們時，他們已經忘了其中7個或8個字了；一個禮拜後，他們還記得的字也許只剩下1到2個；一個月後，可能所有的10個單字都已經忘光了。這樣子的情形我已屢見不鮮。以學習的角度來看，「短期記憶」是沒有價值的。更

As any piano teacher or good pianist will tell you, it takes daily practice over a period of several years. And real professional pianists will tell you they never stop practicing and learning. The same is certainly true of learning. In fact, I believe learning a language is far more complicated than learning a musical instrument.

The point being, don't expect to go to class twice a week, put in minimum practice, and then be able to speak English fluently after 6 months.

So what is a realistic goal?

For the average elementary school student, mastering one or two words a day would be a great goal. Many people would wag their heads at that goal. "Only one or two words a day? That's nothing!" Believe me, it's not that easy. Yes, some students can do that with no problem, and if your child has a gift for language, then by all means encourage that child to learn as much as possible. However, in my experience, most students have trouble learning more than 10 words a week (1.5 words a day). At that rate, the student would learn about 500 words a year.

Note: I'm not talking about "quick" memorizing here. I know lots of students who can sit down and memorize 10 words in 10 minutes in order to pass a quiz. But then ask them the next day what those 10 words mean, and they will have forgotten 7 or 8 of them. One week later, and maybe they remember 1 or 2 words. After a month, all 10 have been forgotten. I have seen that happen again and again. Quick, short-term memorization is worthless. Worse yet, it may give students a false sense of accomplishment. The only thing that really counts is long term memory and mastery of the language. And so I repeat, one or two words a day, truly mastered, is a great goal.

Think of English as a staircase. Looking from the bottom up to the fifth

遭糕的是，這樣一來可能會讓學生得到假的成就感。學習語言真正有價值的地方在於「長期記憶」和語言的熟練度。所以我再一次的重複，如果一天可以學習1到2個字－－我指是真正的熟練－－已經是相當不容易了。

把學英文當做是爬樓梯！如果站在地上看一棟5層樓高的建築物可能會覺得它很高。當然如果你想一下子就從地上跳到5樓是不可能的事，但是，如果能一步一步慢慢爬，就像每天學一點英文一樣，長久下來，成果會非常豐碩的。

我們這樣子看吧！如果一個九歲的學生從小學三年級開始學習英文，並能真正落實以每年500個字的速度來學習；他在六年之後會是什麼樣子呢(也就是他國中畢業時)？一年500個字乘上6年就是3000個字，而一個能活用3000個英文單字的人絕對可以用英語和母語人士做適合不同場合的對談。除此之外，他也已經可以讀許多不同題材的英文刊物；這包括大部份的兒童故事書、基礎的雜誌和報紙。當然，他可能會遇到不熟悉的單字，但就算是程度再高的人都會遇到他們所不熟悉的英文字彙。

付出付價

若真有心想學好英文，你必須要準備好付出付價。雖然說買教材一定要花一些錢，但這裡所謂的代價並不單指金錢方面的花費。以我自己身為一個教師來說，這裡的代價指的是所付諸的努力和時間。另外，考慮「時間+努力」這個因素。一般父母很少考慮到這一點，更不用說是學生自己本身了。就如我上面已經提到的，學習一種語言需要花很多時間，更需花很多努力。

當一個小孩子開始唸小學時，家長會預估這個小孩在六年後完成學業。可是這裡的「六年」所代表的意思是什麼呢？難道是指一個禮拜去學校三

floor seems like such a long way. "It's so far. Can I do it? It's too hard!" You can't jump from the first floor to the fifth floor. However, you can go up step by step. A little bit of work, a little English every day will guarantee that you reach the fifth floor.

Let's look at it this way. If a 3rd grade, 9-year-old student begins studying English and can really master 500 words every year, where will he be in 6 years (at the end of junior high school)? 500 words a year spread out over 6 years means 3000 words. Any person who has mastered the 3000 most basic words in English can easily hold a decent conversation with people around the world. He should be able to read a wide variety of English materials, including most children's stories, basic magazines and newspapers. Of course, there will always be some unfamiliar vocabulary, but that's true at almost any level.

Pay the Price

You must be ready to pay the price, and I'm not just talking the financial cost. Of course, you will have to spend some money. Books and other materials cost money. Teachers will want to be Paid for their time and effort. But what is more important is considering the Time + Work element. Many parents don't consider this carefully, and almost no children do. As mentioned above, learning a language takes time. It also takes work.

When a child starts elementary school, the parent expects it will take 6 years for that child to finish elementary school. But what is entailed in that 6 year time frame? Does that mean 1 hour a day for 3 days a week? Of course not! As everyone knows, children are expected to attend 5 days a week, and for anywhere from 4 to 8 hours a day.

天，一天上一個小時課嗎？當然不是！每個人都知道，小學生一個禮拜要去學校五天，每天都要在學校待四到八個小時。

在前面我曾提到一個「六年學3000個單字」的例子，然而這3000個字不會像變魔術一樣突然的被學會。就好像是你如果放一本英文字典在你的枕頭下，英文單字會自己爬到你腦子裡去嗎？當然不會！想把英文學好時，你必須付出時間和精力！

那要花多少時間呢？我建議學生每天花20到30分鐘來練習英文。這個方式最好的做法就是每天固定一段時間(如7:00到7:30)為英文學習的時間。這段時間可以是在早上、中午或是晚上，重要的是每天的這一段時間都應花在學習英文上。

這就是我所謂的目標和時間表的具體做法。就像做一個上班族，每天上班的時間都是固定的，每天也都有處理固定份量的工作，員工也就照著這個標準來上班。因為如果不能照著做，就有被開除的危險。看看以下這個關於某工作的描述：

一、工作時間：想來上班時再來上班；

二、工作內容：沒有什麼真得需要做的；做任何你想做的；

三、優渥待遇和月休15天；

當然你不可能找到一個這樣子的工作，因為沒有一個老闆會去雇這樣子的員工。英文學習當然也是一樣；除了時間、精力的付出，耐心也是不可或缺的。你必須要很勤勞及很有毅力才能成功。

許多人都知道擁有良好的英文能力可以受用終生，但是每一天投資20到30分鐘來學英文很困難嗎？聽起來，一天20到30分鐘好像不是很多時間，但奇怪的是大多數的學生都沒有辦法做到。

Above, I mentioned the example of learning 3000 words in 6 years. But does learning one to two words a day just magically happen? If you put a dictionary under your pillow, will the words slowly seep into your brain? Of course not! You must do the work. You must put in the time.

How much time? I recommend my students assign 20 - 30 minutes every day to practice English. The best way to do that is to set aside the same period of time every day. It doesn't matter if it's morning, noon, or night. What's important is that some time every day is spent in practicing English.

That's the whole idea of goals and deadlines. If I have a job, and I have to be there at 8 am every day, and I have to do a certain amount of work every day, then I will do it. If I don't, I risk being fired. Look at this job description:

A. Come to work any time you feel.

B. No real project goal. Just do something.

C. Good pay and nice vacations.

What kind of job would this be? What would ever get accomplished? The same is true in language learning. It takes time, it takes work, and it takes patience. You must be diligent and determined to succeed.

Is an investment of 20 - 30 minutes a day very much to learn a language that can serve you for the rest of your life? That doesn't seem like much time, but strangely, I have found few students who can do it.

It takes dedication, but few people have dedication. And the reason few people have dedication is that most people don't keep their goals in front of them. If there is something you really, really want, you will do what's necessary to get it. If you really want to learn English, you will find 30 minutes a day to learn it.

If you want to learn English, you will have to pay the price. You will have to work to win.

學英文需要持續力，而這也正好是大多數人所欠缺的東西。原因在於很多人沒有辦法把目標放在他們面前。如果你真的渴望想把英文學好，你才會肯一天花半小時來做這件事。

如果你真得想學英文，你必須付出代價，你必須準備花許多的心力在這一件事情上面。

我敢這麼說，是十八年來憑著我在許多不同國家，教不同學生的經驗累積。除此之外，我也是以一個爸爸的立場這樣說。我自己有兩個女兒，一個在中國北京出生；另一個則出生在台灣澎湖。也就是說，他們都是在一個全中文的環境裡出生，唸的也是一般台灣的國民小學，她們在家裡和媽媽說的也是中文。可是，她們的英文程度卻不輸給美國小孩。怎麼可能？原因在於我堅持他們每天花20到30分鐘練習英文。我要求我的大女兒每天提早起床，她上學之前和我讀20到30分鐘英文。至於小女兒，她每天回家之後我陪她讀20到30分鐘英文。如果我的女兒們是在同年紀開始學英文（我知道很多家長有2到3個小孩同時開始學英文），那我就會用同一個時間和他們練習英文。

一天花20到30分鐘的時間，長期下來，想學好任何語言都是沒有問題的。這一點在「營造全英語學習環境」這一章中我們會有更詳細的探討。

本章重點：

一、設定目標！不設定目標注定失敗！

二、設定目標時要用很明確的字眼。如：一天學會兩個字；六個月學完這本書。

三、不要設定遙不可及的目標。

四、準備好要付出代價。

I'm speaking from 18 years of experience, teaching English in many different schools, cities and countries. I'm also speaking from personal experience. I have two daughters. One was born in Beijing, China. The other was born on a small island of Taiwan. They have spent their lives in Chinese language environments and attend Chinese language schools. They speak Mandarin at home with their mother. So how's their English. Like an American child. How can that be? I insist they study English every day for about 20 to 30 minutes. For my older daughter, we get up a little early in the morning and read English for 20 to 30 minutes before she goes to school. For my younger daughter, we read English for about 20 minutes after she comes home from school. If they had started studying English at the same time (I know many parents who have 2 or 3 children who begin learning at the same time), then I would have them study together.

20 to 30 minutes properly spent each day will virtually guarantee success in learning a language. We'll look more into this in the chapter titled Creating an English Environment.

To review:

A. Set goals! Having no goals guarantees failure.
B. Make your goals clear. Two words a day? Finish this book in 6 months?
C. Make your goals realistic.
D. Be ready to pay the price.

個人英文學習目標表

Your Goal Form

填完以下這個表，在填每一個選項時都請謹慎地思考再決定。填表時只需在每一個你所要選的選項中打勾，每一行都可複選。舉例來說，如果你覺得你的小孩一個禮拜學習二個小時或三個小時就可以學得好，那就在第二項「學習時間」的2和3打勾。

1	學習重點	□文法	□會話	□閱讀	□全方面語言	□其他______
2	預定達到語言程度	□基礎會話	□通過國內考試	□通過國外考試	□通過升學考試	□其他______
3	上課時間(小時/每周)	□2小時	□3小時	□4小時	□5小時	□其他______
4	學習年限(年)	□半年	□1年	□3年	□6年	□其他______
5	學校類型	□家教	□非專門語言學校	□專門語言學校	□密集課程	□其他
6	師資類型	□中籍英文教師	□外籍教師	□中外籍各半		
7	預估花費(每月／新台幣)	□1000-1200	□1200-1900	□2000-2500	□2500以上	

Look at the table below. Consider carefully all the options. When you are ready, fill in the table by simply putting a check mark in the related boxes. You can place more than one check per line. For example, if you think your child would do well in a program offering either 2 or 3 class hours a week, then check both boxes "2" and "3".

1	Focus	☐grammar	☐conversation	☐reading	☐full language	☐other
2	Competency level	☐basic conversation	☐pass national exam	☐pass international exam	☐pass entranch exam	☐other
3	Class time hours / week	☐2	☐3	☐4	☐5	☐other
4	Time frame (years)	6 months	1 year	3 years	6 years	☐other
5	School *	Private tutor	Non-specialized language school	Specialized language school	Intensive progran	☐other
6	Teacher	local	foreign	foreign and local		
7	Cost / month(NT$)	1000 - 1200	1300 - 1900	2000 - 2500	over 2500	

補習班的種類有很多。很多補習班(或安親班)還提供其他科目的學習(如數學、國語、作文、美勞......)，我把這一些學校歸類為「非專門語言學校」。這裡所謂的「專門語言學校」指的是只提供英文的補習班而言。當然還有其他補習班或機構會提供學生時數較長的學習；在這邊我們把它們歸類為提供「密集課程」的學校。

當然，上表所列選項的選擇可能會間接影響其他選項。舉例來說，如果你一個月只願意花1000元在英文學習上，那麼你就不太可能找一個可以一個禮拜提供5節課的課程。又如果你學習英文的目的只是為了加強自己的口語能力，那麼你可能就不需要計畫要通過某些特定的考試(如全民英檢)，因為通過這些考試往往需要有一定的閱讀和寫作能力。此外，有外籍老師上課的補習班的，學費往往會比只由中籍英文教師執教的補習班來的貴一些。在為自已訂定一個實際的目標時，這些細節都應該被考慮進去。

當你完成上表之後，你就可以準備開始替孩子找一個合適的課程。找補習班時，一個很有效率的方法是查查電話簿的分類廣告，或是詢問自己的親友住家附近是否有合適的課程。但如果你想要一個更詳盡的學校名單，可以上當地縣市政府的教育局網站，找到已經向有關單位註冊的學校名單，同時知道這些學校所提供的課程為何，甚至於是這些學校有沒有聘用外籍教師。

* There are a great variety of schools. Many children's schools that operate as after-school programs offer a broad range of subjects (math, Chinese, school homework, etc.), so these are considered "non-specialized." Schools that exclusively teach English are here labeled "language school." Finally, some schools and organizations offer special intensive programs which may have students studying for 3 or more hours every day.

Notes:

Of course, a decision in one area will affect decisions in the other areas. For example, if you only want to spend NT$1000 / month, then it's highly unlikely you'll find a program offering 5 class hours a week. If the goal is only conversational English, then there is no need to plan to pass a national exam which requires reading and writing. Most programs offering foreign teachers will be more expensive than classes taught only by local teachers. This all falls under the category of making realistic goals.

When you are finished with the Goal Form, you are ready to start looking for an appropriate program for your child. One of the quickest ways is to look in the phone book and ask some friends for their recommendations of what schools are in your area. For a more exhaustive list, go to the Education Department of your local government. They keep lists of all registered schools, and usually have some information about what kind of programs these schools offer and whether they hire foreign teachers.

如何找到一個優良的外籍英文老師

How to Find a Good Foreign English Teacher

這一章所要談的內容和下一章「如何找一家優良的英文補習班」有關且有些重複。但因為在同一所學校裡面的老師有好有壞，而且有些家長可能也希望語言學校以外的地方找老師（如找英文家教），所以我把這個部份獨立出來。

首先，先問大家一個讓人傷腦筋的問題：「為什麼專業的外藉教師在亞洲會如此不足？」

為什麼專業的外藉教師在亞洲如此不足？

要誠實的回答這個問題，我可能會冒犯一些人－－這些人就是和我的職業一樣－－英文老師。但是因為這一本書是寫給有心讓孩子學好英文的家長，所以，以誠實為出發點，我可能會冒犯甚至激怒一些老師或是補習班的所有人。

準備好要了解一些有關英文教學的殘酷事實了嗎？

至少90%以上在亞洲所謂的「英文老師」都沒有經過專業的英語教學訓練。

很快想一下以下這個問題：「如果有一間學校，裡面的老師都沒有受過教學的專業訓練，你會把你的小孩子送到這一所小學(或是更高層級的學校)嗎？」我很清楚我的答案－－絕對不會。

然而，信不信由你，如果在替小孩找外藉教師的過程中，你沒有多作一點功課，幫你小孩上課的可能就會是很不專業的老師。

Some of the points in this chapter overlap information you will find in the next chapter on finding a good English school. But since you may find both good and bad teachers in the same school, and since some parents want to find a teacher outside a foreign language school (for example, a home tutor), this information is presented separately.

First, I would like to address the thorny question:

Why is there a paucity of professional foreign teachers in Asia?

To honestly answer this question, I need to step on some toes—those of my fellow English teachers. But this book is being written for parents who want the best English experience for their children, so in order to be honest, I need to be a little bold and risk the anger of some teachers and school owners/administrators.

Are you ready for the first tidbit of truth?

At least 90% of "English teachers" in Asia are not professionally trained to teach English.

Here's a quick question, and think about it for a moment: would you send your child to an elementary (or higher) school if you knew the teachers were not trained to teach their subjects? I know my answer - I certainly wouldn't!

Well, believe it or not, that is what you will probably get if you don't do your homework when finding a foreign teacher for your child.

Let me repeat: at least 90% of "English teachers" in Asia are not professionally trained to teach English.

讓我再重複一次：至少90%以上在亞洲所謂的「英文老師」都沒有經過專業的英語教學訓練。

你可能會說：「當然，有些私人的英文家教沒有受過英語教學的訓練。但，你不可能是指所有的外藉英文教師吧？」不幸的是，這正是我的意思。

現在你可能會這樣想，「那麼，現在這麼多私人英文補習班裡的老師到底是什麼來歷？或者甚至一些在大學裡的外藉英文講師？」

讓我們回頭來看另外一個更重要的問題：

「什麼樣的人會來亞洲教英文？」

這問題的答案可以讓我們更清楚了解這個問題。以下所列出來的原因也許不是最詳盡的，但絕對已經涵蓋了大多數外籍人士來亞洲教授英文的原因。

一、剛畢業的學生

也就是大學畢業的社會新鮮人（可能來自美國、加拿大、英國等國家）剛開始找工作。他們在大學可能主修任何科目，但絕大多數都不是英文，而且有接受過英語教學訓練者更是少之又少。

二、文化愛好者

這些人被亞洲文化深深吸引，而想要藉著在亞洲居住或旅行來體驗不同的文化。對這些人而言，有著一張外國人的面孔是他們就業的保證，而他們也因而得以體驗不同的文化。

三、被就業市場淘汰者

有些人是在他們所屬的西方國家中無法穩定工作，或者是由於某些原因造成的失業者（也許是在人格特質上有些問題，甚至是酒精和藥物濫用者）。

四、傳教士

Maybe you're thinking, "Sure, I can understand those private home tutors not being trained. But you can't possibly mean all the foreign English teachers!"

Yes, that is exactly what I mean.

At which point, you may be wondering, "So then, who is teaching at all those private language schools? And in the colleges?"

Well, let's take a step back and ask perhaps a more important question:

Who comes to Asia to teach English?

The answer to that will help us gain a better understanding of this problem. The following list may not be exhaustive, but it certainly includes the vast majority of individuals.

A. Recent graduates

Students who finish college (in America, Canada, England, etc.) and are out looking for a job. They may have a degree in any subject, but most likely it's not in English, and rare is the one who has been trained to actually teach English.

B. Culture buffs

Those people who are enamored of Asian culture and want to experience the world by traveling and living in Asia. For them, having a foreign face is a ticket to a job, which then allows them to experience the culture.

C. Washouts

Certain individuals who have a hard time holding a job, or who lost their job in the West, which may stem from personal problems (emotional or personality problems, alcohol or other drug addictions).

D. Missionaries

People who come to spread their religion, and teaching English affords both an avenue into the culture and an income.

E. Professionals (very few)

Those people who have trained to be English teachers because that's what

也就是為了宣教的目的而來的一批人；教授英文除了讓他們得以和當地文化接觸外，更提供了經濟上的支柱。

五、專業英語教學人員（極少數）

接受過專業英語教學訓練的一批人，而從事英語教學正是他們所喜歡做的工作。

由這些原因所產生的結果為何呢？答案似乎是淺而易見的，大多數這些所謂的外藉「老師」在教學上表現不佳（因為他們缺乏適當的訓練，而有一部份人更對於他們所從事的英語教學工作沒有興趣和熱忱），所以往往擔任英文老師的時間不會持續很久。對學生而言，這當然不是個好消息。

那麼又為什麼只有這麼少的專業英語教學人員來到亞洲呢？和許多不同的行業一樣，這個問題和整個市場的狀況有很大的關聯。大體而言，相關的市場問題可以被分成以下兩大類：

一、需求

在亞洲有太多人想要學英文了（小孩、大學生及其他工作上需要用到英文的人），而專業英語教學人員的人數無法滿足這個需求。我們來看看以下這些數字：所有「大中華地區」（中國大陸、香港和台灣）、日本、和南韓的人口加在一起大約就有15億人口。我們假設這一些人當中只有百分之一的人想和外藉老師學英文（而實際上想學英文的人口比例是更高的），那也就是一千五百萬名「學生」。如果以一個外藉老師平均教50個學生來看（當然有些老師教的學生不只這麼少，可是在一些課程中，有些老師只教15～30個學生而已），那麼外藉老師的需求量就高達30萬人！舉例來說，一個訓練英文老師機構網站的統計數字顯示：「每個月就有超過2萬個英文教學相關工作的廣告被刊登出來」。這是很多的工作機會！但問題是，並沒有那麼多的美國人、加拿大人或其他以英語為母語的人士，想要成為專業的英文教學

they want to do.

So what is the result? That's not too hard to guess. Most of these foreign "teachers" do a poor job (because of lack of training and/or lack of interest and dedication) and they usually stay only a short time. This, of course, results in a bad situation for students.

Why do so few professionals come to Asia? As with most any business, much of this problem has to do with market conditions. Fundamentally, the market problems can be broken into two main categories:

A. Demand

There are so many people in Asia who want to learn English (children, college students, businessmen and professionals) that there simply are not enough professional English teachers to meet the demand.

Let's crunch a few numbers. Calculating just the populations of "greater China" (PRC, Hong Kong, Taiwan), plus Japan and South Korea, comes to around 1.5 billion people. Let's say that just 1% want to learn English with a foreigner (the actual percentage should be higher) = around 15 million "students". If the average teacher has 50 students (obviously, some teach more, but there are also many programs where a teacher will have only 15 - 30 students), then that would require 300,000 foreign English teachers! For example, one website for an organization that trains English teachers states: "over 20,000 ESL teaching jobs being advertised each month". That's a lot of jobs! The problem is, there just aren't that many Americans, Canadians, etc. who want to become professional English teachers and then run overseas to find a job.

B. Compensation

Believe it or not, the pay for teaching English is not so great.

Of course, many people in Asia think that English teachers get great pay. For example, the government of Taiwan in 2003 announced a plan to hire a large

人員，並離開自己的國家到別處去找工作。

二、以工作報酬而言

信不信由你，教英文的待遇並不是很高。

當然，在亞洲的人可能會覺得英文老師的待遇很好。舉例來說，台灣政府在2003年宣佈，要從海外聘請老師到公立學校擔任英文老師。很多台灣人看到政府將提供給外國老師的月薪高達70,000到90,000台幣（美金2,000～2,600）時都很驚訝。許多人抱怨薪資訂得太高了，尤其台灣的老師反對聲浪最大，因為他們的平均薪資也不過約50,000台幣而已。我猜想這些提出反對意見的老師之所以反對，是因為他們不想要有外國老師加入競爭市場。以現實的角度來看，任何行業中的大多數人都不喜歡競爭。

然而，我們更仔細的來看看這一些數字。一個月美金2,000～2,600真得是很高的薪資嗎？以我的故鄉（加州）而言，一個專業的老師月薪約為4,000美金。而且，台灣政府聘請這些外藉老師時並沒有打算支付他們退休金（而在台灣或美國的正式老師是有退休金制度的）。除此之外，外藉老師離開自己的國家到另外一個國家定居要另外花費許多錢。再者，他們的工作是沒有保障的。這些老師的工作合約可能只有一年，而隔年就必須找新的工作了。因此，一個月70,000元台幣的薪水看起來就似乎就不是很多了！

因此，台灣政府到現在收到來自專業英文教師的申請不多也就不會出乎意料之外了。相反的，摩門教會對於這個消息卻表示了高度的興趣，也許希望藉著這機會，他們可以讓更多的傳教士到學校去傳揚他們的宗教。

另一個需要考慮的因素是，在以英語為母語的國家裡也有許多教授英語的工作機會。舉例來說，在美國，有數以千計的工作機會是提供給專業的英文老師來教授移民或外國學生英文。既然這些工作所提供的待遇是較好的，而且老師又不需要離開自己的國家（這不僅在經濟的考量上是較理想的，這

number of foreign English teachers to work in public schools. Many people in Taiwan were amazed at the pay package, which came out to NT$70,000 to $90,000 per month (US$2,000 - 2,600). Some people complained that was too much money. Especially some Taiwan teachers complained, since the average pay for teachers in Taiwan is around NT$50,000. And I'm guessing some of those complaining were local English teachers who didn't like the idea of foreign competition. Let's be honest, few people or businesses welcome competition.

But let's look a little closer at the figures. Is US$2,000 - 2,600 per month a good salary? Where I come from (California), a professional teacher makes on average $4,000 per month. This does not take into account that the Taiwan government was not offering any retirement compensation (which the local teachers, in both Taiwan and America, receive). In addition, how much money will American teachers lose by leaving their homes to travel overseas and set up a new home? Additionally, these jobs are not guaranteed. A teacher could be hired one year and then out looking for a new job the next. Suddenly, that NT$70,000 looks very very small, indeed! It's no surprise that the government, to date, has received very few applications from professional English teachers. In fact, one group that immediately jumped on this opportunity was the Mormon church, probably hoping to place some missionaries in the schools of Taiwan where they could spread their religion to students and parents.

Another point to consider—there are many English teaching jobs in native English countries. For example, in America, there are thousands of jobs for professional English teachers to educate immigrants and foreign students. Since those jobs offer better pay and benefits, and do not require a person to leave his country (financial cost plus personal emotional costs of leaving home, family, friends, and familiar culture), many professional teachers opt to remain in their

些人也不需要離開自己的家人、朋友和熟悉的環境），這也就是為什麼許多老師還是選擇留在自己國家工作的原因。

我們很快的複習一下：

1、薪資低（相較之下）

2、較少的福利（如無退休金）

從這裡我們也許就可以知道為什麼很少專業的英語教學者會來亞洲了。既然沒有足夠的專業師資來到亞洲，許多學校在沒有機會找到好的老師時，也就只好接受沒有專業資格的老師了。

你準備好要了解更多殘酷的現實了嗎？

許多外籍英文老師的母語根本就不是英文。

更不幸的是，有許多英文補習班的經營者認為，補習班只需要這些外國面孔來吸引學生。而以一般的情形而言，這卻是事實！許多學生和家長如果看到一個白種人，就會很自然的以為這個人的母語是英語。但是事實上，我曾遇過很多來自世界各國的「英文」老師，而在這些國家中，英文並非他們的母語。關於這一點在下一章中我會談到更多。

有些學校根本就不在乎他們老師的母語是不是英語。

開英文補習班是做生意，而做生意當然就是為了要賺錢。如果一所學校沒有辦法（或者不想花太多錢）聘請專業的英文老師，而補習班經營者也認為家長可以接受非英文母語人士來當老師，那麼補習班當然就會雇用他們手邊能找到的外國人。在多數情形下，他們所能找到老師的母語並非英語，而他們所拿到的薪水往往也就比較低了。

home countries.

Let's do a quick review:

a. Low wages (in comparison)
b. Few if any benefits (like retirement)

Perhaps we can see why few professional teachers will come to Asia. Since not enough professional teachers want to come to Asia, schools have to struggle to find good teachers, and will therefore accept unqualified people.

Are you ready for the second tidbit of truth?

Many foreign English teachers are not even native speakers of English.

Unfortunately, many school owners think that all they need is a foreign face to attract students. And in many cases, that's true! Students or parents see a white face and assume the person is a native English speaker. In reality, I've met "English" teachers from a wide variety of countries where English is not the native language. I'll go into more detail in the next chapter.

Some schools don't even care whether their teachers are native speakers.

A school is a business. The business exists to make money. If a school cannot find (or doesn't want to pay for) professional English teachers, and the school owner thinks parents will accept non-native speakers, then the school will hire the people who are available. Many times, the available people are non-native English speakers, and they are usually cheaper to hire.

既使大多數英文老師沒有接受過英語教學的專業訓練，他們絕大多數不想接受訓練，而大多數的學校也不提供師訓。

如果你還記得我們上面提到的「誰來亞洲教英文」，那麼這一點就不是很難理解了。對於許多以教英文為生的外國人而言，即然這個工作並不是他們想一生從事的行業，他們自然不會想在這一方面做專業的成長了。既然沒有得到專業的訓練且缺乏興趣，結果往往是：只要能拿到薪水，這些老師是不會想在工作上有太多突破的。再加上許多學校沒有提供教學法的訓練，或者只是讓老師接受熟悉他們所要使用教材的基本訓練，結果當然就是品質不良的教學隨處可見。

讀完以上這些內容後，我很怕很多家長已經準備放棄尋找一個好的外藉英文老師了。當然不必要有這樣子的想法！這些並不是我真正想說的重點。反而，我希望大多數的讀者可以了解到這些是我們目前所必須面臨的問題。我希望你們可以了解在全亞洲的現實狀況為何，而一旦了解了這些問題之後，你就應該要尋找出一個解決的方案。以上是我們希望你能避免掉的錯誤，現在我們來談談一些比較正面的事情。

何謂一個好老師？

我們已經談了許多何謂一個不好的老師，現在我們來看看如何才能找到一個好的老師。

你可能會這麼猜想，好老師的評量標準就是壞老師的相反。但事實上問題並沒有這麼簡單。除此之外，我不想要讓讀者認為任何一位被我們歸類為

Even though most English teachers are not trained to teach, most of them don't seek training, and most schools don't offer training.

If you remember the table above of "Who comes to Asia to teach English?" then you'll see why this is true. For many foreigners who take jobs teaching, since the job is not a professional career decision, they are not very interested in professional development. With little or no training and minimum interest, the consequence is a teacher who will do the least he has to in order to get paid. And since most schools either don't offer pedagogical instruction, or offer only the minimum training necessary to get a teacher familiar with materials and methods, the result is poor quality all around.

After reading the above, I'm afraid the average parent is ready to give up on finding a good teacher. No! That's not what I'm trying to communicate. Rather, I want to make the reader well aware of the problem we face. I want you to be clear about what the real situation is all over Asia. Once you are aware of the problem, you are better prepared to face the problem and find a good solution. All of the above is to help you know what to avoid. So now let's move on to the good stuff.

What is a good teacher?

We've noted some things that make for bad teachers. Now let's see how you can find a good teacher.

As you might guess, a simple measure of a good teacher might be just the opposite of what makes for a bad teacher. In fact, it's not quite as simple as that. Additionally, I don't want to leave the reader with the impression that all those who fall into the categories listed above in "Who Comes to Asia to Teach

「誰到亞洲來教英文」的人就是不好的老師。舉例來說，有些大學剛畢業的學生、文化愛好者或者是宣教士都可以成為不錯的老師。

所以，我們來看一下一個好的英文老師所擁有的特質有哪些？

一、教育背景和專業訓練

這狀況是因人而異的。一個老師是不是英文、語言學或相關領域的主修？這個老師有沒有受過專業的訓練？許多擁有英文教學碩士學位的老師會在大專院校或一些特別的課程中授課。另外一個較普遍的則是「英語教學證書」，但要特別小心的是，和碩士學位不同，證書沒有特定的標準。也就是說，一張證書可能代表的是良好的訓練，也有可能代表一點訓練都沒有。有一些所謂的「證書」只是一張從網路上買來蓋滿印章的廢紙。然而，有些卻是訓練的證據。舉例來說，我在1987年時所受的訓練是長達7周整天的訓練，課程內容包括課堂教學、評量，以及實際教授剛到洛杉磯地區的移民英文。當你在評量一個老師時，仔細的尋問有關他們所受過的訓練。記得，你是消費者，也就是付錢的人，你有權利知道你的老師是不是受過專業的英語教學訓練。如果英文補習班和老師拒絕回答相關的問題，這通常就有問題了。

二、是否為英文母語人士

正如我已經提到過的，你會聘請一位美國人來台灣教小朋友中文嗎？法國政府為聘請一個日本人到巴黎去教法國小孩法語嗎？當然不會。既然如此，如果可以找到一位英文母語人士時，為何要聘請非英文母語人士呢？這問題的答案似乎很顯而易見的，可是很多家長在尋找英文老師時卻常忽略。在儘可能的狀況下，找英文母語人士來當英文老師。

English?" will be poor teachers. For example, there are some recent college graduates, culture buffs, and missionaries who make fine teachers.

So let's consider some characteristics of a good foreign English teacher.

A、Education and professional training

Comes in many forms. Does the teacher have a degree in English, linguistics, or a related field? Has the teacher received professional training? Most teachers who earn the MA in TESL (Master of Arts in Teaching English as a Second Language) go to teach at colleges or in specialty programs. There is another, more common "Certificate in TESL". The problem is, unlike a Master's Degree, there is no standard for a certificate. In other words, a certificate may mean either good training or almost no training at all. Some "certificates" are merely pieces of paper with a stamp that are purchased over the Internet. However, some are proof of true training. For example, the program I trained under back in 1987 was full time, lasted 7 weeks, and included classroom instruction, testing, and practical experience teaching immigrants in the Los Angeles area. When you are evaluating teachers, ask careful questions about their training. Remember, you are the customer; you are paying money; it is your right to know whether the teacher is qualified to teach. If the school or teacher refuses to answer or avoids these questions, that usually means trouble.

B、Native English speaker

As noted, would you hire an American to teach Mandarin to children in Taiwan? Would the French government hire a Japanese lady to move to Paris in order to teach French children the French language? Probably not. So why hire a non-native speaker to teach English if you can find a native teacher? This seems so obvious, and yet so many parents overlook it when finding an English teacher. Whenever possible, try to learn from a native speaker.

三、教學經驗

對任何行業而言，經驗會讓一個人表現得更出色。一位有經驗的老師通常比較知道學生的問題在哪裡、如何解決學生的問題、了解如何組織並計畫課程、引導課堂上課氣氛且和學生的相處往往也較融洽。

四、過去教學紀錄

一個最簡易和最好評量一位老師的方法就是觀看這位老師過去的教學紀錄。這位老師的學生表現如何？他們在各項英文比賽中有得名嗎？他們通過任何國家級的考試了嗎（如：台灣的全民英檢或是國際公認的托福）？

五、學習及專業成長的動力

任何一位老師，無論多麼有經驗，都應該有學習的慾望，因為學習是無止盡的，而且永遠都會有方法可以讓一位老師的教學更好。以我個人的經驗而言，過去四年來，我所用的教材和我的教學方法已經改變了許多。為什麼？因為我一直找到更好的教材，而我的太太則會指出我教學上的缺失。當然，有時候改變並不是很有趣的，但是為了要成為一個更好的老師，我們必須願意且隨時準備改變。

六、精力

找一位在課堂上總是充滿精力的老師。一位無精打采的老師往往也就會教出無精打采的學生。而一位充滿活力、在課堂上和學生打成一片的老師，會讓課堂充滿活力、並幫助學生把注意力放在學習的事務上。

七、幽默感

就像精力一樣，一位幽默的老師可以幫助學生更專注在課堂上，並讓學習的過程充滿樂趣。

C、Experience

As with most any profession, experience helps. An experienced teacher will usually be better at identifying and solving problems, organizing and planning curriculum, guiding the class atmosphere, and relating to students.

D、Track record

One of the simplest and best measures of a teacher is to look at the track record. How have the teacher's students done? Have they won English contests? Have they passed national-level tests? (For example, in Taiwan, the GEPT, or for international standards, the TOEFL.)

E、Desire to learn and grow

Any teacher, no matter how experienced, should want to learn more. There is always more to learn, and there are always ways to improve. A personal example: both the curriculum I use and the methods I use to teach have changed greatly over the past 4 years. Why? I found better teaching materials, and my wife pointed out weaknesses in my teaching style. Oh, sometimes it's not fun to change! But to become better, we must be willing and ready to change.

F、Energy

Look for a teacher with lots of energy in class. A slow, lethargic teacher will usually produce slow, lethargic students. A teacher who is up, moving, and having fun with students will keep the class full of energy and help to focus the students on learning.

G、Humor

Like energy, a teacher with a good sense of humor will help to keep students focused in class and make learning more fun.

八、變化性

一成不變往往就代表著無趣。老師如果可以增加課堂的變化性往往更能捉住學生的注意力，同時提供學生不同方式的學習機會。我有一個基本的原則：以一堂一小時的課而言，至少要包括三個以上不一樣的活動。一般而言，如果學生的年齡愈小，他們相對的英文程度也就愈低，而就需要更多的變化性。所以，找一位上課充滿變化、且知道不同年紀學生有不同需要的老師。

九、教學熱忱

如學生有特別的需求時，老師是不是願意幫忙呢？如果學生在某個方面有學習上的困難時，老師是不是願意多花時間輔導學生呢？如果學生想參加某英文考試或競賽時，老師是否願意花額外的時間協助和訓練學生呢？這些都是教學熱忱高的老師會有的特質。

十、有長期教學的準備

學習一種語言通常都要花上許多時間。既然如此，你會想要和一個兩個月後就準備離開的老師學習嗎？所以，在找老師時，了解一下該老師準備在當地居住多久。時常更換老師的學生往往到後來學習效果都不是很好。

十一、找一個會說中文的老師

這和我們如上所提到第二和第十點項的道理是一樣的；找老師時，最理想的狀況就是找到一位母語是英文，而且已經住在台灣一段時間的老師。因為住在台灣已經一段時間了，這位老師也就應該會說中文，而這一點會讓老師和家長及小孩子溝通時更順利。

H、Variety

Monotony is a great fountain of boredom. A teacher who displays creativity by adding variety will help to hold students' attention and give learners the opportunity to learn in a variety of ways. I have a general rule: for every hour of class, there should be at least 3 different distinct activities. In general, the younger the class and the lower the English level, the more variety is needed. So look for teachers who incorporate variety into their lessons and who are aware of the diverse needs of students who are at different levels and different ages.

I、Dedication

Will a teacher help with special needs? If your child is having trouble in a certain area, will the teacher take time to help? If students want to join a special test or enter an English contest, will the teacher give the students extra coaching and practice? These are all marks of dedication in a teacher.

J、Long-term commitment

It takes time to learn a language. Do you want to start class with a teacher only to have him/her leave after 2 months? When looking for a teacher, ask how long the teacher plans to be in your area. Most students who often change teachers end up learning very little.

K、Bilingual

Remembering points B and J above, clearly one of the best individuals to find in Taiwan is a native English speaker who has lived in Taiwan for some time, so that he/she understands the culture and also speaks Mandarin. This can aid enormously in communicating with parents and children.

十二、整潔的儀容

就我本身而言，我並不喜歡太過正式的穿著。我不喜歡穿西裝，尤其討厭打領帶。然而，通常一個懂得注重儀容的老師會比較尊重自己和他人。一個看起來不整潔或衣著隨便的老師可能在做事上也會比較隨便。

從以上所談到的這十二點，你大概已經清楚一個好的老師所該具備的條件到底有哪些了，所以你也就知道你應該尋找怎麼樣的老師了。當然你不太可能找到一位在這12個項目中都表現很好的老師，然而必須提醒你的是，如果降低自己的標準後，您的孩子的學習經驗往往可能不會是很好的。我把這十二點做成一個評分表，你可以使用這做表來評量一位老師。

根據你想要評量的老師填寫下表，然後把所有的總分加起來你會得到0到36分中的一個分數。當然，分數愈高就代表這個老師愈好。我個人建議以下列的分法來評量一位外藉老師：（低於20分=可能不是一個很好的選擇）

30-36分=優異

25-29分=很好

20-24分=不錯

但對於剛從大學畢業的學生可能有格外注意。舉例來說，假設有一個剛從大學畢業的加拿大學生，他有英語教學的證書，然後他到台灣來教英文。由於他完全沒有經驗，所以他可能在評分表中只能拿到18分。然而，他有可能在日後成為一位很好的老師。因此，評分表所得到的分數不應該是評量一位老師的唯一依據。

L、Appearance

Personally, I'm not a stickler on formal appearance. I hate wearing business suits, and especially ties. However, a neat, clean appearance shows a certain fundamental respect for self and others. A teacher who looks unclean or sloppy may prove to be careless in other areas.

From the above 12 points, you can gain a fairly good understanding of ingredients found in a good English teacher. Now you know what to look for. You probably won't find high marks in all 12 categories in any one teacher, but at the same time, if you allow your standard to become too low, your child will probably not have a good learning experience. Let's put all 12 points into one form, which you can then copy and use to evaluate various teachers.

By filling out the form with either checks or writing the point values on each line, then adding up all 12 categories, you will get a score between 0 and 36 (12 x 3). Of course, the higher the score, the better. I would suggest the following evaluation scale for grading foreign English teachers:

30 - 36 = excellent

25 - 29 = very good

20 - 24 = good

under 20 = probably not a good choice

The one caveat here would be a new graduate. For example, let's say a Canadian student graduated from university, received a certificate in TESL, then came to Taiwan to teach. Because of no experience, he might only achieve a score of 18. However, he might become a very good teacher. Therefore, this evaluation form should not be applied too rigidly.

教師評量表

老師姓名: ____________

得分	3分	2分	1分	0分
教育背景 &專業訓練	□英語教學 碩士	□大學語言相關 科系畢業	□英語教學證書	□其他
是否為英文 母語人士	□是 能力很好	□不是，但英文 能力不錯	□不是，但英文	□不是
教學經驗	□超過5年	□3-5年	□1～2年	□少於6個月
過去教學紀錄	□學生通過一些 重要考試	□學生在英文 比賽中得獎	□老師有不錯的 教學聲望	
學習及事業 成長的動力	□發表個人英語 教學著作	□擔任英語教學 師訓講師	□參與相關 教學訓練	□無
精力	□上課是讓人興 奮的	□充滿活力的 充滿活力的	□大致上是	□上課無精打采
幽默感	□常常	□有時	□偶爾	□很少

Teacher Evaluation Form

Teacher name: ____________

Point Value	Excellent	Very Good	Good	Poor or Not
	3	2	1	Applicable - 0
Education & Training	MA in TESL	BA in English or Linguistics	Certificate in TESL	other
Native English speaker	Yes	No, but superb English	No, but very good English	No
Experience	Over 5 years	3-5 years	1～2 years	> 6 months
Track record	Students pass major exams	Students win contests	Good reputation in community	
Desire to grow*	**Writes ESL materials**	**Speaks at ESL conferences**	**Attends ESL seminars**	**None**
Energy	Exciting	High energy	Good energy	Lethargic
Humor	Often	Sometimes	Occasional	Rare

變化性	□常常	□有時	□很少	□沒有
教學熱忱	□總是充滿教學熱忱的	□時常充滿教學熱忱的	□有時	□沒有
有長期教學的準備	□接下來的2年(或以上)都準備從事英文教學工作	□準備教學1-2年	□1年	□沒有長期教學的打算
是否會說中文	□中文流利	□中文不錯	□有基本中文溝通能力	□不會說中文
儀容	□優異	□很好	□不錯	□不好

Variety	Great	Some	Little	No
Dedication	Always	Usually	Sometimes	Never
Commitment	Over 2 years	1-2 years	1 year	None
Bilingual	Fluent	Good command	Basic communication	None
Appearance	Excellent	Very Good	Good	Poor

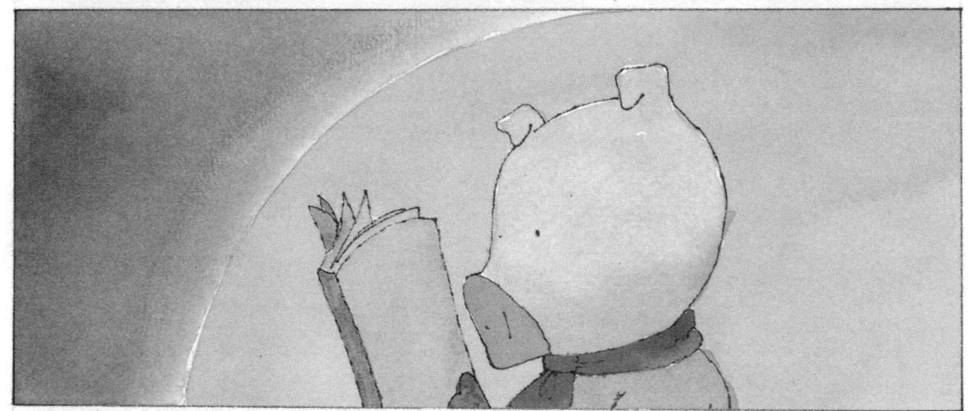

如何選擇一家專業的美語學校

How to Choose a Professional English School

老師和美語補習班老闆

雖然這個題目在之前已經討論過了，但前一章的重點在於家長找外藉英文老師時所應該注意的地方，而這一章的重點則放在美語學校本身。

因為沒有足夠的專業英文老師願意來到亞洲任教（原因我們在上一章已經有深入的探討過了），美語補習班也就很難找到好的老師。因此，大部份學校都會採取以下其中之一的做法：

一、雇用有「外國面孔」的老師。

二、雇用符合最低基本需求（但這些需求和英語教學並不相關）的外國人。

三、雇用外國老師並給予基本的訓練。

待會我們會再花一點篇幅來討論以上這三種作法。但首先，我們先來探討這一個很重要，但卻往往被忽略掉的問題：這些美語補習班的老闆到底是哪些人？以一些坊間的小型私人美語補習班而言（也就是指亞洲大多數的學校，包括一些連鎖的語言學校），美語補習班的老闆就是當地的生意人。只有少數的美語補習班老闆自己本身是英文老師，如果是外藉老師自己所開設的美語補習班那更是少之又少。絕大多數的美語補習班老闆都是把美語補習班視為是賺錢工具的生意人。即然是做生意，我們就試著來瞭解一下他們的心態。

一個生意人決定要開一家美語補習班時，他首先面對的第一個決定就是他要設立的是獨立的美語補習班，或者是要加盟其他體系的補習班。如果他決定要設立一所獨立的美語補習班，那他就要面對許多美語補習班都會面臨到的問題－－找老師。而如果他決定要加盟其他體系的美語補習班，那麼總公司方面往往可以幫忙解決找老師的問題。

 Teachers & School Owners

Although this topic has been discussed, the last chapter focused on what parents should be aware of when looking for an English teacher. This chapter is written from the viewpoint of evaluating English schools.

Because not enough professional teachers want to come to Asia (the reasons for this problem were discussed in some depth in the last chapter), schools have to struggle to find good teachers. Most schools take one of the following options:

A. Hire any "foreign" face they can find

B. Hire a foreigner with basic (but irrelevant) requirements

C. Hire foreign teachers, and provide some basic training

In just a moment we'll take a closer look at these various options, but first, let's consider a fundamental question that is rarely asked: who are school owners? For small private English schools (which means most of the schools in Asia, including most of the chain schools), the owners are simply local businessmen. A few may be English teachers, and a very few may be foreign English teachers who have opened their own schools, but the vast majority are just businessmen who see an English school as a way to make money. It's business. So let's take a moment and try to understand their situation.

A businessman decides to open a school. The first choice he has to make is whether to open an independent school or a franchise. If it's an independent school, then he'll have to solve the biggest problem that all English schools face —how to find English teachers. If he joins a franchise, then the franchise headquarters will usually take care of that problem.

So what does the independent school owner do? Usually, he has two options:

所以，開設獨立美語補習班的老闆他會怎麼做呢？通常他有兩個選擇：一在報紙或網站上刊登廣告找老師，或者透過相關的人力仲介公司找老師。在亞洲，隨便打開一份英文報紙都可以看到徵英文老師的廣告，我偶爾會關心一下類似的訊息以了解相關的現況為何。但這樣子的方式對一個生意人來說是個既苦又長的過程，特別是如果他自己本身的英語能力不好時。想像一下就知道了，這些生意人刊了廣告之後，有些有興趣的外藉老師打電話來尋問相關的訊息，可是這些生意人卻無法和他們溝通，這對這些生意人來說就是個難題了。因此，很多生意人只好透過人力仲介來完成這項任務，而透過人力仲介卻往往代表著另一層的剝削。

為了要獲利，人力仲介公司必須儘可能的仲介最多的人數。他們如果不是自行在當地刊登廣告，就是和國外的仲介公司合作（如加拿大或南非），而也因此要和這些國外的仲介公司平分所賺得的費用。仲介公司往往不負責找來優良、受過專業訓練的老師；基本上，他們所負責的的是找到合乎最低要求，並且願意接受他們安排教學工作的人。

就另一方面來談，如果一個生意人決定加盟其他體系的補習班時，他就不需要花時間在找老師這問題上面。加盟體系的補習班往往都是由公司總部負責找老師的工作，而這個部門往往也是公司裡最忙碌的部門之一。為什麼呢？因為大部份的外藉「老師」在台灣停留的時間不會超過一年。

不論一個生意人是透過仲介公司或是透過加盟補習班的總公司來找老師，對於你們這些想要幫孩子學好英文的家長們，結果往往都是相同的－－也就是找到不會停留很久的非專業老師。這又是為什麼呢？因為不論是獨立的或是加盟體系的美語補習班，他們很少是想找專業的英語老師（我們在前一章已經談過了外藉老師的福利問題和供需關係）。他們真正想尋找的是，以花費最少的前提下，學生和家長都能接受的老師。這樣一來，他們即可以

1) place ads in English newspapers or on websites that help locate teachers, or 2) work through a professional recruiting agency. If you open any English newspaper in Asia you can usually find ads for English teachers. Once in a while, I look through these ads just to see what the current situation is. But this process can be long and difficult for a local businessman, especially if he/she lacks good English skills. Imagine this: the owner places an ad, some foreigners call to ask about the job, but the owner cannot communicate with them. There's an obvious and immediate problem. Therefore, many owners work through a recruiting agency, which is another layer of business.

In order to be profitable, recruiting agencies need to process a large number of teachers, and to maximize profits, as many teachers as possible. They either advertise in the local market, or have relationships with overseas agencies (like in Canada or South Africa) with whom they have to split the fees. Recruiting agencies are not responsible for training teachers or even guaranteeing that the teacher is good and professional. Basically, they are just responsible for finding a person with the minimum requirements who is willing to come and teach.

If, on the other hand, a businessman decides to join a franchise, most of his concerns regarding finding teachers will be relieved. Large franchise chains all have central offices to handle the problems of finding teachers. And those are usually busy offices. Why? Because most foreign "teachers" rarely stay for more than one year.

Whether a businessman works through a recruiting agency or a franchise operation, for you, the parent of the child wishing to learn English, the result is basically the same—an unprofessional teacher who stays for a short time. Why? Both independent schools and franchises rarely look for professional teachers. (The problems of supply-and-demand and low wages were covered in the last chapter.) What they want is someone the parents and students are willing to

達到學生和家長的需求，同時又能把成本降到最低，進而獲得最多的利潤。這也就是「教育是為了要賺錢」導向下的現實狀況。

那麼美語補習班最後雇用了哪些人呢？誰願意千里沼沼的跑到亞洲來做一份低薪資、低福利的工作呢？上一章我已經由「供應者」，也就是老師，的角度來回答這個問題。現在我們再以「需求者」，也就是美語補習班，的角度來看這個問題。我們現在來看之前所提到學校找老師時的三個選擇：

一、聘請有「外國面孔」的老師

有些學校選擇老師只因這個老師會講英文及有一個外國面孔。美語補習班老闆認為他們只需要這些外國面孔來招攬學生（或是愚弄家長？）。然而，這些老師中有些人的母語根本就不是英語。我這樣說可不在開玩笑，因為我自己就遇過許多「英文」老師，而他們卻是來自義大利、法國、匈牙利、德國等等國家。有些人會來到這裡的原因是因為經濟不景氣而他們需要工作，而有些人則只是想在他們旅行時有一份差事可以賺錢。因為歐洲的學校體系往往都要求學生修六年以上的英文，所以這些西方人大多數都會講英文。

現在有一個狀況如下：一個亞洲的生意人想要雇請一個會講一點英文的外國面孔來他的學校任教；如果你是他你會怎麼做呢？你有兩個選擇，你可以一年花約35,000美金（或甚至更多）來請一位專業的英文老師，或者是花18,000美金請一位俄國人（或是看起來像外國人的其他國家的人）。而如果學生不知道如何分辨老師的好壞，或者是學生家長不在乎而沒有進一步的去了解，補習班老闆選人時當然就不會太用心了。對大多數生意人來說，他們的目的是為了要賺錢，所以也就不難了解他們會雇用哪一種老師了。

平心而論，如果這一類的老師英文能力還不錯，再加上適當的訓練之

accept at the least possible cost to the business. In this way, they can satisfy the requirements of the parent and/or student, and keep costs to a minimum, thereby maximizing profits. That, quite simply, is business in the English "education for profit" world.

So whom do they end up hiring? Who will come to Asia and work for low wages and low benefits? The last chapter answered this question from the "supply" side, the teachers. Let's turn it around and answer from the "demand" side, the schools. We shall now take a closer look at the above-mentioned three options schools take in finding teachers.

A. Hire any "foreign" face they can find

Some schools choose a teacher only because he/she can speak some English and has a foreign face. School owners think that all they need is a foreign face to attract students (and perhaps fool parents?). However, many of these teachers aren't even native English speakers. I'm not joking. I personally have met "English" teachers from Italy, France, Hungary, Germany, and the list goes on. Some of these people are coming from depressed economies and need work, while others may just want a source of income while they travel the world. Since most European countries have school systems requiring at least six years of English, these white Westerners all speak at least some English.

So here's the situation: a businessman in Asia needs a foreign face and a little English in his school. What would you do in his shoes? You have a choice. Either you hire a professional native speaker for about US$35,000 per year (or more), or you get a Russian (or any other national who could pass as a native speaker) for $18,000. And if the students don't know the difference and the parents don't care enough to ask, is this a difficult choice? For most businessmen, the goal is making money. This kind of choice was already made.

後，他們是有可能成為不錯的英文老師。但我還是不會把我自己的小孩送到這樣子的美語補習班去。以一個關心學生教育的家長的立場為考量點，如果我可以找到一位優良的英文母語人士來當孩子的老師時，為何要退而求其次呢？

我們再從不同的角度來看這一個問題。如果你是一位住在台北的學生家長，你會把你的小孩送到美國學校去學中文嗎？假設有一位美國人已經在台灣住了10年，中文講得很好，讀寫能力也不錯，你會花很多的錢來請這位老師教你的小孩中文嗎？答案是淺而易見的，當然不會！你會請台灣當地的老師，也就是母語是中文的老師來教你的孩子。這裡的重點就是，如果你可以找到一個很好的英文母語人士來當英文老師時，這當然會是最好的選擇。

二、雇用符合最低基本需求（但這些需求和英語教學並不相關）的外國人

在一般的狀況下，政府要求各學校只能雇用符合某些資格的人當英文老師。這出發點當然是好的，但我們來看看政府所訂定的「資格」是什麼。一般而言，這些所謂的資格只不過是「大學畢業」。我想我們政府的官員大概覺得只要一個人能讀到大學畢業，他就可以教英文了。那是不是同理可證，台灣的大學畢業生（無論主修為何）都可以在台灣的學校教中文了嗎？我可不這麼認為。

別認為在大專院校裡情形會好一點！的確，大學在聘用老師時的要求是較高，因為依規定，所有台灣的大專院校只能聘任擁有碩士以上學歷者擔任老師。但一點還是要特別注意，碩士學位可能代表的是任何學位！意思就是說，很多大學聘請有學位的「英文」老師，可是這些老師所拿的學位卻不是英文，這些老師大概也沒有受過英語教學的訓練。舉例來說，離我家不遠的地方就有一所技術學院，他們所請的外藉老師是有碩士學位沒錯，可是他的

In all fairness, some of these individuals speak decent English, and with proper training, they might make good teachers. But I would certainly have reservations about sending my children to such a teacher. And as a caring parent, why would I if I could find a good native-English teacher?

Let me flip the coin for you and we'll look at the question from a different angle. If you are a parent of a child and you live in Taipei, would you send your child to an American to learn Mandarin Chinese? Let's say that American had lived in Taiwan for 10 years and spoke good Mandarin, and could read and write some. Would you hire and pay high wages to that American to teach your child Mandarin? Answer: of course not! You would hire a local, native-Mandarin speaking teacher. My point being, if you can find a good native-English speaking teacher, then that's naturally preferred above any other choice.

B. Hire a foreigner with basic (but irrelevant) requirements

In general, schools are required by the government to only hire teachers who fulfill some basic requisites. That sounds good, but let's dig a little to find out what these "requisites" are. In almost all cases, the requirement is simply "a college degree". I guess the government figures that if you can obtain a college degree, you can teach English. Does that mean that any Taiwan national who obtains a college degree (in any subject) is qualified to teach Mandarin in the schools of Taiwan? Hmmm, I don't think so.

And don't think that the universities are any better! Yes, their requirements are higher. Colleges are only allowed to hire teachers who have obtained a master's degree or some proven equivalent. But here's the catch—that degree can be in any subject! What that means is that many colleges hire "English" teachers who have degrees, but not in English, and they probably have no TESL (Teaching English as a Second Language) training. For example, there is a col-

主修是藝術！那麼他有什麼資格來教英文呢？答案是沒有。

這就好像是我修完了歷史碩士，是不是代表我現在可以到專科以上學校去教物理了呢？當然不是！但不幸的是，很多人都跳脫不出「學位」的迷思，即使是一些高級知識份子也不例外。讓我再告訴你另外一個例子。

我以前認識兩位在同一個縣市的同一地區工作的外藉女老師，她們兩位的母語都是英語而在當地都有很不錯的聲望。其中一位是大學英文系畢業，並且有受過英語教學的訓練；另一位則是拿了某種心理學的碩士學位。我知道的情形是，當家長考慮要幫他們的小孩子找一位英文老師時，如果要從以上所提到的這兩位老師其中選擇一位時，大多數人會選擇第二位老師。為什麼？因為她有碩士學位！對這些父母來說，不管是不是和英文教學有任何關係，只要是碩士就一定比大學畢業的好。

如果把這個邏輯用在別的事物上時，你就會知道這其實是很荒謬的。如果車子壞掉了，我應該請我的哥哥來修理，為什麼？因為他是微生物學的博士，他一定比那些連高中都沒畢業的修車廠員工來的厲害，不是嗎？嗯，再看看下面這個例子？有人結婚想請客！恭禧恭禧！那麼打電話給那位教藝術的教授吧，為什麼？即然他的學位比較高，他辦喜宴的能力一定比這些餐廳員工要來得厲害！

如果有人是這樣子做事情，你一定會想說他如果不是瘋了，就一定是個蠢蛋；而他的確是。可是在英語教學的世界中，大家卻覺得這是很正常的。

三、雇用外國老師並給予基本的訓練

既然能雇用到的外國老師都沒有接受過專業的訓練或沒有經驗，那麼另一個解決的方法就是提供老師在職訓練。通常，只有大型的美語連鎖補習班才有時間、設備、人員及教材來提供他們老師訓練之用，而有些補習班在這一方面的確做得很不錯。除了職前訓練之外，老師開始任教後補習班還會有

lege right across from my house. The foreign teacher they hired does possess a master's degree - in art! So what qualification does he have to teach English? None.

If I receive a graduate degree in History, does that qualify me to teach Physics at the college level? Of course not! Unfortunately, many people are blinded by "degrees," even people who should know better. Allow me to give you an actual example.

I know two foreign teachers who work in the same area of a city. Both are native speakers and are fine ladies with good reputations. The first received a bachelor's degree in English and obtained TESL training. The second received a master's degree in an area of psychology. I was told that a group of parents was considering where to send their children to learn English and that these two teachers were at the top of their list. Whom did these parents choose? The second teacher, of course. Why? Because she has a master's degree! To them, it doesn't matter that the master's degree has nothing to do with teaching English.

Let me apply this kind of logic to other areas of life and we'll see how it works. I suppose if my car breaks down, I should take it to my brother to fix. Why? Well, he has a doctorate in microbiology, and that's better than the car mechanic who barely graduated from high school. Right? Hmmm. How about another one? We're having a wedding party! Congratulations! Call the art professor. Why? Well, he has a high degree, so can do a better job catering than the restaurants. Okay.

If someone acted like that, you would either call him insane or stupid, and rightly so. But in many areas of the English teaching world, that is considered normal.

C. Hire foreign teachers, and provide some basic training

後續的訓練課程。

然而，許多學校是不提供這樣子的訓練的。而對於身為家長的你來說，如何分辨美語補習班給老師做的訓練品質好壞或數量是否足夠是有困難的，因為這些美語連鎖補習班看起來都差不多，而這些補習班也都宣稱他們有給老師做師訓。

有一次，一位來自加拿大的女老師來我的補習班應徵，她先前在某家「知名」的美語連鎖補習班工作。我問她為什麼想離開那家補習班，她說她很討厭那個補習班的老闆。她看了我們補習班所用的教材後，馬上就說：「這些書比我們用的書好太多了！我真希望我們也可以改用這些教材。」我再問她關於補習班提供給老師的「職前訓練」時，她說那根本就是個笑話。我再請教她有關後續的師訓時，她回答：「有啊，他們上禮拜才剛來過；他們來看我上課。」「然後呢？」我問：「他們有沒有給妳任何回饋啊？給你一些建議或改進的方向？」「沒有，他們看完就離開啦！」

這竟然就是一些補習班所認為的後續師訓，這些負責做師訓的員工如果不是沒有能力，就是太不負責任了。無論是哪一種情形下，對於身為父母的你要找出提供老師完整師訓的美語補習班都是很困難的。

而當然，學校還有第四個選擇

四、聘請專業的外藉老師

但是就如我們上面已經討論過的，極少數的學校會做這樣子的選擇。那既然如此，家長該怎麼做呢？這是關乎你的小孩和你所要繳的學費。如果我打算為我的孩子找一所美語學校，我會做以下這三件事情：

1. 詢問該補習班任用老師的標準：他們雇用怎麼樣的老師？我的目標是找一個母語為英語、曾受過英文教學訓練且有教學經驗的老師。

Since most of the foreigners available for hire are untrained and inexperienced, one solution is to provide on-the-job training. Usually, only the large chain schools have the time, facilities, personnel and materials to offer training for their teachers. A few chains actually do a good job in this, providing both initial preparation and regular follow-up evaluations and continued training.

However, many do not, and it is particularly difficult for you, the parent, to discern which are the better ones, since the chain schools usually look the same and most of them will claim to provide training.

One day, I had a Canadian lady come to my school to ask about getting a job. She was working at a large "famous" chain school in Taiwan. I asked her what was wrong and why she wanted to work for me. She said she hated her boss, the businessman-owner. She looked at the books I use in class and immediately responded, "These are so much better than the books we use. I wish we could change to these." I asked her about the training the chain school offered, and she said it was a joke. I asked about the follow-up training. "Yes, they just came here last week," she responded. "They watched me in class." "So," I continued, "did they offer any feedback? Some ideas or suggestions for improvement?" "No, they just watched and left."

That is what this chain considers to be continueding training. Maybe they just have a really incompetent or irresponsible training staff. In any case, it could be quite difficult for you, the parent, to discover which chains offer the best training.

Of course, the last option is for schools to

D. Hire professional foreign teachers

But for the reasons already discussed, very few schools will opt for this.

So what are you, the parent to do? It's your child and it's your money. If I

如果這一所學校沒有這樣子的老師，那麼就到別家學校去問問看吧。

2. 打聽一下某間補習及該校老師的聲譽如何：但不要相信你所聽到的一切，因為很有可能的狀況是以訛傳訛。然而如果一間學校長久下來已經建立了很不錯的聲望，那可能該校的辦學真得不錯。
3. 要求試聽：學習一種語言需要花很多的時間，所以你準備付出的將是時間和金錢上的投資。而也因為如此，你有權利試聽以了解上課的情形為何。一所好的、負責任的學校也應該可以公開坦白的來讓你試聽。事實上，我甚至鼓勵我學生的家長到我的課堂上來一起聽課，這樣他們就會知道我上課的內容和他們孩子學習的狀況為何。

教材和教學方法

雖然這方面的探討感覺上會是滿枯橾的，但教材和教學方法的重要性是再怎麼強調都不為過的。選擇合適的教材，加上老師正確的引導，可以讓身為家長的你省下很多金錢，更可替你的小孩子省下許多時間，而達到較好的效果。也許你不相信我，讓我以下面這個例子來印證我的論點。

這是發生在我和我學生身上的實例。不要以為我是在吹噓，寫這件事的目的在於更清楚彰顯我的論點。由於這些都是我自己的學生，我可以證明，也敢保證這些都是真實發生的事情。（如果你不相信，我有報紙的剪報為證）

慎選教材，並使用正確有效的教學方式，再加上努力的學生，得到的結果會是如何呢？當然效果會很好。坊間大部份的美語補習班要求學生一個禮拜上3個小時或甚至時數更長的課，而我補習班的學生一個星期則只上二2

were looking for a school, I would do three things:

a. Go to the school and ask about the hiring policy. Who gets hired? My goal is to find a native-English speaker with training in teaching language and some experience. If the school doesn't hire such people, then I should look elsewhere.

b. Ask around about the reputation of the school and the teachers. Don't believe everything you hear, or it could be a case of the blind leading the blind. But if a school has built up a good reputation over a period of years, that is one positive indication.

c. Ask to sit in on one or two classes. Learning a language takes years, so you are about to make a major investment in both time and money. You have a right to see what you're getting, and good, responsible schools should be open and honest, willing to let you see what you're paying for. In fact, I encourage parents to come to my classes. I want them to see both what I'm doing and what their kids are doing.

Materials and Methods

Although this topic may sound boring, I cannot overemphasize the importance of methods and materials. The proper choice of materials and the methods teachers employ to present the materials can save you, the parent a great deal of money and the student, your child an immense amount of time, and achieve better results. In case you don't believe me, let me give you a quick but very true example.

This example is taken from my own life and regards my students. I'm afraid you will think I'm bragging, but I'm writing this only to very clearly illustrate this point. Since these are my students, I can verify and guarantee the truth.

個小時的課。坊間補習班除了要學生一個禮拜花更多的時間上課之外（換句話說，超過在我自己補習班上課時數的1/2），他們通常也比較貴。在這種情形之下，坊間美語補習班的學生一周上課的時間較多（約多了50%），付的學費也較貴（大約也貴了50%左右），所以他們在各項英文競賽和英文考試的表現應該會比我的學生好才是，但結果呢？

在國去五年縣內的各項英文競賽裡，我學生（以平均數而言）的表現一直都比其他學校來得出色許多，而通過英文考試（如全民英檢）的比例也比較高。事實上，兩年前我們當地的一所技術學院也派了一群學生去考全民英檢。提醒你一下，台灣大多數的大專院校學生，不論是在學校或在外面補習班，學英文的時間都至少超過六年。而我部份的學生同時也參加這一次的考試（他們學英文的時間大概只有3至4年）。結果技術學院的學生通過本次考試的比率只有40%；而我的學生呢？他們大多數都只是國中、國小的學生而已，通過率卻有80%，高出全國平均通過率兩倍之多。

沒錯，這些都是真實的數字。我希望你沒有讀到睡著了，現在我再強調一次：慎選教材，並使用正確有效的教學方式，再加上努力的學生，這樣子所得到的學習效果才會是最好的。

記得我先前提過那一位很喜歡我補習班教材的女老師嗎？一般英文連鎖補習班的教材有一個很大的缺點，就是他們只用他們自己的教材。這倒也不難理解，因為賣書給學生，補習班可以賺很多錢，所以即使市面上有更好的教材，大部份的美語連鎖補習班還是不會考慮採用，因為出版自己的教材可以為他們賺進許多錢。他們在意的是所能賣出教科書的數量（當然也就是利潤的高低），而非教科書的品質。

那麼，替連鎖美語補習班寫這些書的人又是誰呢？你做好心理準備了嗎？答案是……通常都是由非專業甚至非英文母語人士所寫的。似乎很難相

(Anyone who doesn't believe it can check newspaper reports. I have kept the clippings.)

Just how much difference can the proper choice of materials and the correct employment of effective methods combined with dedicated students make? A huge difference. While most private English schools have students attend class for 3 or more hours a week, the majority of my students come for only 2 hours/week. Not only do most schools teach for 3 or more hours/week (in other words, 50% more than I do), they are also more expensive than mine. Given this fact, that students in other schools attend more hours of class every week (50%) and pay more in tuition (also about 50% more), they should do much better than my students both in standardized tests and in general English competitions. So what's the truth?

In countywide contests, for the past five years, my students (taken as an average) have always done better than students from other schools and have gone on to pass nationwide standardized tests (like the GEPT) at a much higher rate. In fact, two years ago the local college sent a group of students to take the GEPT. Let me remind you, most college students in Taiwan have studied English for 6 or more years, both in the public schools and in outside private classes. At the same time, a group of my students (who had studied for 3 or 4 years) took the same test. The result? The college students had a pass rate of 40%. My students, who were mostly junior high school and elementary students, had a pass rate of 80%, more than double the national average.

Yes, those numbers are correct. I hope you're awake now so that I can repeat: the proper choice of materials and the correct employment of effective methods combined with dedicated students can make a huge difference.

Remember the teacher I mentioned above who came to my school, looked at the books I use in class and immediately responded, "These are so much bet-

信，不是嗎？我認識一位在台灣某家知名英文連鎖補習班總部工作的美國人，他告訴我說這家補習班會用他的名字出版一些不是由他寫的書藉。為什麼要這樣子做呢？既使某些書是由台灣老師寫的，補習班喜歡在作者欄的位置裡填上外國人的名字。這樣一來，會讓人以為這些書都是外國人寫的，不但可以討好家長，補習班也因而可以賺很多錢。

身為一位學生家長，我很厭惡這樣子的行為。如果再以一個英文課程編寫者的身份，這樣子的行為更是讓我憤怒。

而在這種情形下，你和你的小孩所必須付出的代價為何呢？假設你的小孩從小學三年級開始學英文一直學到高中畢業，也就是大約十年的時間。你每個月付$2500元的補習費，一年就要花掉約$30,000，或者說十年內要花掉$300,000（這還是在沒有通貨膨脹的狀況下）。加上這十年內所要花的時間，不計算孩子年紀小時你必須接送他們去補習班，你的小孩要花約1500個小時在課堂內。

你曾從這個角度來思考過問題嗎？如果選擇不慎，你所要付出的代價將是$300,000元和超過 1,500個小時的浪費。不得不慎重一點啊！

也許你現在會覺得我太誇大其詞了！花了十年學英文怎麼可能是浪費呢？我舉另外一個實例。三年前，有家長帶著他們當時唸小學的孩子來到我班上，這位學生在「私人家教補習班」（也就是學校老師在家裡所私設的家教班）學了兩年英文。兩年後，他的父母希望他能轉到我這裡來上課。我幫他做了測試後發現，他的英文程度幾乎是零，而必須從我學校最初級的班重上，這個結果當然讓這位學生和他的家長大吃一驚。一年前，他的父親和我聊天時感嘆的說：「當初怎麼會浪費了那麼多時間和金錢呢？」之後他謝謝我，因為當時他的兒子在我班上英文已經進步了很多，而且成績相當不錯。

這不是一個個案，我常常會遇到像這樣子的學生。幾乎每個月我都會接

ter than the books we use"? One problem with chain schools is that they are virtually tied in iron chains to their curriculum. You see, there is a fantastic amount of money to be made by selling books to students, so even if there are better books on the market, most chain schools won't even consider them because they make so much money by publishing and selling their own materials. Their main interest is quantity (of profit), not quality.

And who writes the materials for chain schools? Are you sitting down? The answer is... usually non-professionally trained individuals and often non-native speakers. Hard to believe, isn't it? I know one American who worked in the head office of a large and famous chain school in Taiwan. He told me that the company would often put his name on materials he didn't even write. Why? They needed to put foreigners' names on the books even though Taiwanese authors were writing them. That way, it would look like foreigners were writing their English curriculum...to make the parents happy...to keep the money flowing in.

As a parent, that really irks me. As an English curriculum writer, that gets my blood boiling.

And what is the cost to you and your child? Let's say your child begins learning English in the 3rd grade and continues until graduating from high school. That's 10 years. If you pay NT$2500 each month for 3 hours, that would work out to $30,000 per year, or $300,000 for 10 years (assuming there is no inflation). Add to that all the time—in the earlier years, you probably take your child to and from the classes, plus about 1500 hours spent by your child in class.

Did you ever think about it that way? A poor choice could mean wasting $300,000 plus over 1500 hours of lifetime. Think about it.

Perhaps you feel I'm exaggerating too much. How could 10 years of learning English be a waste? Here's a true-life example. I had an elementary school stu-

到已經在其他補習班學二年、三年、甚至四年的插班生，而他們的英文程度幾乎是零。當然，別誤會，並不是每一位來我補習班插班的學生都像這樣。坊間還是有很多很好的學校，但同時也有太多良萎不齊的美語補習班。

要不要再聽聽另一個例子啊？五年前，本地縣政府辦了一個兒童說英文故事比賽，並聘請三位評審評分。來自各不同英文補習班，超過五十名學生報名參加國小低年級組的比賽。結果呢？我的學生包辦了一、二、三名。你可能又會覺得我再吹噓，但這不是我的重點；這裡的重點是，好的教材、正確的上課方式和努力的學生，三者加在一起時，才能得到最好的效果。

如果想更進一步了解如何選擇一家英文補習班的教材及教學法時，請參看前一章「英文學習簡介」。

dent and his parents come to me three years ago. He had studied for about two years in a "house school," you know, some local "English teacher" who holds classes in his or her home. So after two years, the parents brought him to me and asked to have him join one of my regular classes. After testing him, I discovered that he knew virtually no English and would have to start in a beginning class, which was a big surprise and something of a disappointment for both the boy and his parents. About a year ago, his father was talking with me and he shook his head, saying, "How could we have wasted so much time and money?" Then he thanked me, because his son had by that time learned so much and was doing very well.

But you see, I run into students like that all the time. Almost every month I have students come to me who have studied for two, three, even four years, but who know almost no English. Please, don't misunderstand. Not all students who come to me are like that. There are good teachers and good schools out there. But there are also far too many bad ones.

How about another example? About five years ago, the county held a contest for children to tell stories in English. A panel of three judges listened to each and awarded prizes. Over 50 students entered the 1st and 2nd grade division from a wide variety of private English schools. Result? My students took 1st, 2nd and 3rd places—all the top prizes. It may look like I'm bragging. That's not my point. My point, once again, is that good materials and methods combined with dedicated students will make a huge difference.

For more notes on what materials and methods to look for in a school, please reference the previous chapter "Introduction to English language learning".

美語補習班的氣氛

「歡迎光臨」是每所好的美語補習班所該有的重要特質。若以一家補習班的氣氛而言，我會從以下兩個層面來做考量。首先，一家補習班的整體環境感覺如何？當你走進一家補習班時，你的整體印象為何？你是受禮遇的嗎？補習班的工作人員（補習班老闆、接待人員、老師）是不是很友善的接待你呢？第二，補習班的上課氣氛為何？學生是全神貫注的嗎？他們是否積極的學習？他們是否一直接受較難的挑戰呢？

當然，讓你的孩子到美語補習班上課的另一個很重要的目的，是讓孩子慢慢建立起使用英文的自信。身為一個家長，你會希望孩子能專注在上課的內容上，而不是注意還剩幾分鐘才下課。你會希望他們在課堂上是需要花費心思及有機會使用他們想像力。學生必須在一個互動良好的班級裡學習最生活的美語，而不斷的被挑戰接受難度愈來愈高的問題。

坊間許多補習班有這樣一個趨勢，外藉老師被要求只能用英文上課。這個作法的理論背景是希望學生能有更多接觸英文的機會，也就是希望在課堂上學生只能接觸到他們所要學的語言，而不要使用學生本身的母語。根據他們的理論，學生會因此「被迫」使用他們所該學習的語言。

這樣子的做法對於可以在全語言環境中上課的學生，也就是一天可以在全英語環境裡上6至8個小時的學生而言效果會很不錯，而這樣子的做法也常常在大學裡被使用。但是如果以一位一個禮拜只能上2-3個小時的小孩來說，這樣子的上課方式對他來說簡直就是浪費時間。因為若採用這樣子的方式，如果要教學生為什麼第三人稱動詞要加"s"（如"I walk"和"he walks"）時，老師可能要花上一個小時不斷的用英文解釋文法和舉例，但是學生卻還是聽不懂老師想說的到底是什麼。然而，如果用學生的母語解釋五分鐘，再

Atmosphere

"Welcome" stands for an essential element of any good school. When I think of atmosphere, two aspects come to mind. First, what is the general environment of the school? When you walk into the school, how does it feel? Do you feel warm and welcome? Is the staff (administrator, secretary, teachers) friendly, open and helpful? Second, what is the ambiance of the class? Are the students alert? Are they actively learning? Are they being challenged?

Of course, one goal is for students to feel ever more comfortable and "at home" in English. As a parent, you hope your child will want to concentrate on the class rather than on the clock. You hope they will throw intellect and imagination into the lesson. Students should be challenged to learn and use common English in interactive settings that gradually become more difficult.

There's a fad going around some schools. Foreign teachers are told to use only English in class. This is based on the language immersion concept, where in language class, students should only be exposed to the target language with nothing in their native tongue. According to this theory, learners will then be "forced" into acquiring the target language.

This works pretty well in total immersion situations, where students are "immersed" in the language for six or eight hours a day, and is also often used in university language courses. But for little children who get only two or three hours per week, much of this kind of class will just be a waste of time. A teacher can stand there and give example after example for an hour or two, accompanied by grammatical explanations in English, of why the third person singular present tense verb has an "s" at the end (i.e., "I walk" vs. "he walks"), but the kids are probably still not going to understand it. However, give me five minutes in their native language with a few examples in English, and they're on

用英文舉幾個例子，學生概念就已經很清楚了。所以啦，小心類似所謂全美語的上課方式。

一個真正學習的氣氛，要在學生的需求和課程的需要中間達到一個平衡。如果老師、課程內容和上課的方式是充滿想像力和創新的，這樣一來學生不但學習興趣被啟發了，學習的興緻也能維持較長的時間。

補習班學生表現紀錄

如同上面已經提到過的，在過去的五年裡，我的學生在全縣的英文競賽中總是能比其他學校的學生表現來得優異，且而請不要忘記，其他補習班的學生一周上超過三個小時的課，我的學生一周則只上兩個小時的課。這就是我補習班過去的紀錄，也正是我的英文課程整體表現的證明。身為一個聰明的家長，你應該要仔細的評估一間補習班之前學生的表現為何。

有另一個例子可以印證這個論點。我的一位學生Mike向我學很長一段時間的英文。高中畢業後，他到桃園去唸大學。我不清楚是不是全台灣所有的大學都會這樣做，不過以Mike的例子來說，他的大學要求所有一年級新生接受一個英文考試。Mike並不是一位很特別的學生，他的資質不算資優，但也不至於愚鈍。事實上，他各方面的表現都很普通。他個性不錯，心地也很善良，我把他當朋友看待。不過，有一點很特別的是，他沒有到其他補習班補習。相反的，他只上過我的正規課程，而大多數在亞洲的大學生至少都曾在英文補習班上過六年以上的課。話說回來，在2001年和Mike上桃園這一所大學的所有新生中，只有七個人通過這個新生英文考試，而Mike是其中之一。除此之外，他在大學裡的英文考試成績時常保持在第一名。他只是我其中之一個學生而已，我還有其他更多的學生。

their way! Be wary of fads.

A true learning atmosphere balances the needs of the students with the goals of the course. A class atmosphere where the teacher, the materials and the methods are imaginative and resourceful will help to arouse and sustain effective learning.

Track record

As mentioned above, in countywide contests over the past five years, my students have always done better than students from other schools. And remember, my students have two hours of class per week, whereas most other schools have three hours. That is a track record, an indication of something about my entire English program. As a wise parent, you should take a school's track record into serious consideration.

Here's another case in point. Mike was one of my long-term students who graduated from high school and went on to a college in Taoyuan. I don't know whether this happens at all universities in Taiwan, but at this particular one, all the 1st year students were given an entrance exam in English. Now Mike is kind of a special student. No, he's not a genius, and neither is he stupid. In fact, in most ways, he is very much average. He has a friendly personality and a very kind heart. I like to think of him as a friend. However, he's special because he never went to any buxiban (cram school). Instead, he just attended my regular class. Most other college students in Taiwan and many areas of Asia go to English cram schools for at least 6 years. Anyway, so of the 200 1st year students at this college in Taoyuan who took this English entrance exam, only 7 passed. Mike was one of those seven. In addition, he has consistently achieved 1st place in his college English tests. That's just one student, but I have many

當考慮送孩子到哪一家英文補習班時，你有權利查閱該家補習班過去學生的表現紀錄為何（事實上，站在身為父母的角度而言，我倒覺得這是你的義務）。這家補習班學生過去的表現如何？他們在各項全國性的檢定考中表現如何？他們在縣內舉辦的英文比賽成績如何？

想一想，如果某家美語補習班的學生過去都沒有很好的表現，你認為你的小孩在這裡會學得很好嗎？假設你的小孩在這間學校表現得很好，那大概也和這間學校沒有太大的關系，而是因為你的小孩資質不錯，那如果是因為你的小孩資質不錯的話，如果到一家規劃更完善的補習班學習時，你的小孩表現還會再更出色。由這一點出發，如果一家補習班的學生表現都一直不錯時，你的小孩到這裡後如果能好好的學習，一定也可以有很不錯的表現的。

但是，要小心作假的紀錄。有些美語補習班會因為學生沒有太出色的表現而去創造學生有良好表現的假象。你可能會想說，這些紀錄怎麼有辦法作假呢？通常他們都是透過以下這三種方式來做：

一枝獨秀型

某些美語補習班可能只有一、兩位資質特別好的學生，而補習班也就只能靠這些學生來博取名聲。

代打型

某位學生可能本來在其他美語補習班就已經學得很好了，而現在看起來會讓人以為新的補習班有良好課程的錯覺。

紀錄作假型

因為有些美語補習班規劃的課程不好，所以他們知道他們的學生不可能通過全國性的英文考試（如全民英檢），他們會自創一些測驗，而甚至給這

others.

When you are looking for a school, you have every right to inquire of the track record (in fact, as a parent, I think it's your duty). How have their students done? Have they passed national standardized tests? Have they done well in countywide contests?

Think about it. If School A can't produce any consistent success, do you think your child will do well there? And on the off chance that your child thrives there, it's probably not because of the school, but rather that your child is gifted and would do even better in a superior environment. In this regard, a school whose students regularly succeed is probably one where your child, properly motivated, will do well.

Beware of false track records. Some schools, because they don't have a good record, will try to create one. You might wonder, how could a school create a false track record? It usually comes in one of three forms:

The Single Star

A school has one or two "genius" students, and relies on its very few successes to give it an appearance of excellence.

The Borrowed Star

A student who has already learned English well at one school moves to another school, so now the new school looks like it has a great program.

The Fake Record

Because some chain schools have poor programs and know their students will never do well on national standardized exams (like the GEPT), they will create a counterfeit test, and may even give the exam a name which is very close to a standard exam. This counterfeit test is specially tailored for their program,

些他們自創的測驗取一個很像其他全國性英文考試的名稱。但這些測驗都是針對某些補習班課程內容設計的，所以在這些補習班補習的學生自然就能考得很好，補習班也就用這樣子的結果來討好家長和學生。這就好像是用假的黃金和鑽金做的一個假戒指，也許看起來還不錯，但卻不是真的。就像假文憑沒有實際用途一樣，這些英文考試的成績也就無法證明任何事情，而只是突顯出他們的英文課程根本就是規劃不良而已。

就因為這些原因，考慮一間美語補習班的學生表現紀錄是有其必要性的。畢竟，這也就是為什麼世界上有些學校會成為名校（如哈佛大學和麻省理工學院），因為他們的教授群都是最頂尖的，而他們的學生也就能成為不同領域的各中翹楚了。

標準要高

你真希望你的孩子英文學得好嗎？我想既然你會唸這一本書，答案當然自然是肯定的。可是，我覺得我還是必須不斷的提醒在亞洲的家長，學英文就像學習其他科目一樣，當你想找一間補習班時，你必須找一間對學生要求很高的補習班。就像你買食物的時候，你會去買快爛掉的蔬菜嗎？如果一間餐廳裡的地板、桌面到處都是食物的殘渣，還有蒼蠅飛來飛去，你還會去那裡吃飯嗎？如果你是正常的一般人，你會義正嚴詞的回答：「當然不會」。而在選擇一家好的美語補習班時，我們難道就不該用同樣的高標準嗎？若以高標準來看補習班，這裡有一些準則和問題是你在選擇一家補習班時要特別留意的。

一、 補習班所在的大樓是否安全？消防安全是否合格？事實上，我知道很多父母甚至不考慮這一點。這太可怕了，如果你的孩子發生

to guarantee that their students will do well. This will make the students and their parents feel good. It's like having a ring made of fake gold and diamonds. Maybe it looks nice, but it's not real. A fake degree has little use. And fake English exams prove nothing—except that the schools, essentially, are admitting that their programs don't really work!

For these reasons, examining the track record of a school is a proper consideration. After all, there are reasons why some universities (like Harvard or MIT) have obtained their distinct and grand reputations—the staff is top-notch and the students go on to succeed in a variety of endeavors.

High standards

Do you really want your child to learn English well? I am supposing, if you're reading this book, that you do. However, I feel that I must constantly remind parents in Asia that, as in so many other areas of life, when you look for English schools and teachers, you need to aim for high standards. When you shop for food, do you want to buy rotting vegetables? Do you like to go to restaurants that have old food sitting on the floor, scraps left on unwashed tables and flies swarming around? If you're like most people, your answer should be a resounding "Of course not!" The same should be true in choosing a teacher or school for your child, shouldn't it? Regarding high standards, here are some basic questions you should keep in mind and ask as you consider schools and teachers:

A. Is the building safe? Does it meet or exceed the fire codes? In fact, I know many parents who don't even consider such questions. My goodness! What good is having your child succeed at becoming a top student if he/she dies in a school

了意外，即使他／她是全國最頂尖的學生又有什用呢？要把每一件事的輕重緩急搞清楚。

二、 補習班的老師是不是有接受過良好的訓練呢？這些老師是不是英文教學領域中的各中翹楚呢？我自己就有遇過一些學校標榜他們是「雙語學校」，可是他們任用的老師卻沒有辦法說幾句英文。如果老師本身的口語溝通能力都這麼差了，他們能教出多好的學生？自己想想吧！

三、 教室的採光是否明亮、舒服，並且是有助於學習的？

請記住，學習英文是一輩子的投資。這也許要花上許多的時間和金錢，但過人的英文能力會為您的小孩帶來更大的報酬。就因為這個原因，為何不將要求訂到最高呢？

fire? Get your priorities straight.

B. Are the teachers well—trained? Is their English top—notch? I personally know of some schools that advertise themselves to be "bilingual schools" but whose teachers can't communicate in English. If the teachers can hardly speak English and have terrible pronunciation, what sort of students will they produce? Think about it.

C. Is the classroom bright and friendly, comfortable and conducive to learning?

Please remember, a good English education is a lifetime investment. It takes a lot of time and probably money, but it will reward your child for the rest of his or her life. Why not aim for the highest standard possible?

營造一個美語學習的環境

Creating an English Environment

 輸入（input）和輸出（output）的概念

無論是學習哪一種語言，無外乎就是聽、說、讀、寫這四個層面。而這其中，聽、讀可以歸類為「語言的輸入」，說、寫則歸類成「語言的輸出」。

在語言學習的過程中，學習者要達到一定的「輸入」之後才能慢慢的產生「輸出」。嬰兒在剛出生時就不斷的接受語言的輸入（聽），等到輸入的量夠多了之後，他們才會慢慢的有辦法輸出（說）。學生也是一樣，在他們有辦法說和寫之前，他們必須要先接受大量的聽和讀。

由這個概念出發，也就不難了解為什麼營造一個英文學習環境有多重要了。如果環境建立得好，學生所得到的輸入（聽、讀）夠多了之後，再加上適當的引導，他們的輸出（說、寫）也才會有所進展。

 全美語環境？

有很多人認為，學美語最好的方法就是讓學習者到一個「全美語環境」去學習，就像小留學生一樣，在一個英文為母語的國家生活久了之後，英文當然也就流利啦！

不可否認的，在任何一個英文為母語的國家（如美國、加拿大、英國等國家）當然就是最佳的英文學習環境。在這種環境下長大的小孩，英文程度當然就可以提昇到和母語是英文的小孩一樣好。可是，為了種種原因（如經濟上的考量），不是每個人都有辦法把孩子送到國外去生活的。此外，有些家長即使有能力送孩子到國外唸書也不見得想這樣子做，因為他們想讓自己的孩子在屬於他們自己的國家中成長，保有自己的文化思想和背景。

當然，處在一個母語不是英文的國家中，要營造出一個百分之百的全美

Concept of input and output

No matter what language you are going to learn, you must deal with listening, speaking, reading and writing. Among them, listening and reading may be categorized as "input" or "reception" of language, while speaking and writing are "output" or "production."

In the process of learning languages, learners must be exposed to a certain amount of input before they can be expected to produce "output." Toddlers are normally exposed to large amounts of listening long before they are ever expected to speak. The same applies to students. If we expect them to produce English (either speaking or writing), they must be exposed to a great deal of listening and reading.

Based on this concept, it is not difficult to understand why creating an English learning environment is very important. If the environment is well developed, students will be exposed to significant input, and with appropriate guidance they will begin to effectively produce English.

All-English environment?

Many people think the best way to learn English is to put learners in an all-English environment, like children who grow up in a foreign country. Once children live in a country where English is the mother tongue, certainly their English will be fluent.

Undeniably, living in any country where English is the mother tongue (United States, Canada, Britain, etc.) affords the best opportunity to learn English. Kids growing up in an environment like this can be expected to learn

語環境的確是有困難的。但如果家長用心的話，即使不能做到百分之百，還是有辦法營造出一個和全美語環境相似的美語學習環境。如果這個環境被營造得好，孩子的英文能力當然也就可以被提昇。

從教導我自己女兒英文的過程中，我歸納出了一些有關如何營造一個良好居家學習環境的具體做法。關於我兩個女兒的學習狀況，我在下一章中會有更詳細的描述。

語言學習的內在條件

在先前的幾章中，我們已經探討過如目標的設定、如何尋找優良的外籍教師和美語補習班等這些有關英語學習的重要議題。但這些內容都是學習語言的「外在條件」。現在讓我們回過頭來看看學習語言的「內在條件」，而我個人更認為這是語言學習中最重要的一個因素。

對於美語補習班所教授的內容和補習班老師所採用的教學方法，家長是沒有辦法做太多干涉的。然而，對於自己家裡的學習環境，你卻有很高的自主權，可是這卻也是很多父母容易忽略掉的一環。

在先前的幾章中，我有提到一些學習成效很好的學生，可是當然也有一些學生的學習成效不是很好。這些學習成效不佳的學生，究其原因，往往可分為二類：一種是學生本身對學習英文沒有興趣（有很多學生會去補習班是因為父母逼他們去；即然他們不想學，他們當然也就不會努力）；第二種則是家庭學習環境不良，而孩子學習成功與否往往就取決於父母所做的決定為何。

如果觀察一位學習表現良好的學生，你會發現，十個學生裡有九個的家長是很關心孩子的學習狀況的。即然如此，家長應該如何積極參與孩子的學

English as a mother tongue. However, it's not practical for most people to send their children to study abroad. In addition, some parents who have the financial means don't want to send their children abroad because they want their children to maintain their own culture and language.

Of course, in a non-English speaking country, it is nigh impossible to create an all-English environment. However, if the parents take certain steps and strive toward this goal, they can create something similar to an all-English environment. If that environment is well organized, the children can obtain an excellent mastery of English.

The following points I write from experience in teaching my own daughters English and trying to create a good home learning environment for them. In the next chapter, I will give a few more details about my daughters.

Learning at home

At this point, we've explored the major topics of language learning, the importance of setting goals, how to find a good foreign language teacher, and what to look for in an English school. Most of this has focused on what to look for and what to avoid "out there." Let us now turn our attention to "in here," what I consider perhaps the single most important factor in effective language acquisition.

You have little control over what a school teaches or what methods a teacher employs. In contrast, you do have a great deal of control over your own home environment. This is a factor many parents overlook.

Earlier in this book, I mentioned many examples of students who have succeeded. But there are also those who haven't done well. In most cases, it was due to either a lack of motivation on the part of the student (many students only

習呢？

1. 營造一個居家的學習環境
2. 和孩子一起學習
3. 讓孩子了解學習是很重要的
4. 孩子表現得好時要給予鼓勵
5. 孩子表現不好時的處罰方式
6. 以正面的態度來解決孩子學習不良的問題

營造一個居家的學習環境

家長有很多營造居家學習環境的方法，以下我們以學習音樂來舉例。假設你想要讓你的小孩喜歡音樂，你會怎麼做呢？以我個人來說，我會在家裡準備各種不同的音樂CD、在家裡常常放音樂、並鼓勵我的小孩讀有關音樂的書籍和偉大音樂家的傳記，我還會鼓勵我的小孩去學習某種樂器。而如果希望孩子接受正統音樂教育時，我更會督促他們每天練習。

我了解到，在現今這個世界上，學習英文比音樂欣賞要來得重要許多。我個人很喜歡音樂，但我也清楚地了解音樂沒有辦法幫助我找到職業、讓我能夠旅遊、經商、與人溝通、使用網際網路、讀國際性的期刊或看懂電影……。然而，以上所提到的這些都是學習英文所能對來的好處。

所以，學音樂和英文哪一樣對我的小孩來說比較重要呢？很明顯的，是學英文要來的重要！

既然如此，該如何幫孩子創造一個居家的學習環境呢？記得上面我提到有關學音樂的例子吧？以下這是一些比較具體的做法：

come to class because parents force them—they don't want to be there and so they put in minimal effort) or a lack of home learning environment. A student's success or failure in learning English is often largely the consequence of decisions the parent makes.

Find a student who regularly achieves top scores on school tests, and 9 times out of 10, I'll show you parents who are actively involved in their child's education. How can parents be positively involved?

a. Create a home learning environment
b. Sit with the child and practice together
c. Help the child understand learning is very important
d. Reward the child for doing well
e. Some form of punishment for failure
f. Find positive steps to address and resolve failure

Create a home learning environment

There are many ways parents create home learning environments. Here's a simple example from music. Let's say you want your child to grow up with a love of music. What would you do? Personally, I would have a variety of music always available at home. I would regularly play music CDs. I would persuade my child to read about music and great musicians. I would encourage my child to choose an instrument and begin playing it. For serious education, I would push my child to practice daily.

Now, I understand in today's world, English is far more important than music appreciation. I love music, but I realize music is most likely not going to get me a job, is not going to help me when I travel, do business, communicate with other people, use the internet, read international periodicals, or watch

一、在家中貼上一些物品的英文名稱

例如：將 "radio" 這個字貼在收音機上面。當然在這樣做之前，你必須要確定你的孩子會讀和說這些字，因為如果你不教孩子如何認讀這些字時，孩子不會對這些字留下任何印象，自然也就不會學會這些字了。

二、讓孩子聽符合其程度的英文廣播或其他有聲教材。

三、聽孩子英文教科書所附的英文CD

這聽起來是理所當然的，可是很多家長卻容易忽略掉。在聽CD時，有一些做法可以讓學習更有效率：

1. 要孩子手指指著課文：

這對年紀小的孩子特別重要，因為如果父母沒有在旁督促，孩子聽CD時很容易就分神了，要求孩子，CD唸到哪手就指到哪可以讓孩子更專注在聽的內容上。

2. 跟著CD做覆誦：

這是另一個可以讓孩子更專注在CD內容上的方法，而且除了孩子專注力更高之外，長期下來孩子的口語能力也會有進步。

3. 聽CD的次數要愈多愈好：

聽CD的次數愈多，當然學生對課文的熟悉度就會愈高。但是和先前提到過「分散學習」的概念一樣，如果同樣是要聽三次，三次分三天聽完的效果一定會比一次聽完三次的效果來的好。

除此之外，聽CD時不見得孩子就要乖乖的坐在桌子前面聽。平常只要有機會，如孩子早上剛起床刷牙洗臉這一段時間、玩玩具的時間都可以利用。其他如車上也可以放一份CD，接送孩子時就可以放給孩子聽。另外，因為既然很多小孩聽CD時會想睡覺，那就幹脆在孩子睡覺前再把CD撥放

movies, and the list goes on and on. However, English will do all that.

What's more important for my child? Obviously, English!

So what can I do to create that home environment? Remember the example of music above? Here's a quick list of simple things that virtually anyone can do.

A. Some parents stick the names on common objects around the house.

For example, stick a little piece of paper that says "radio" on the radio. Of course, make sure the child can read and say the word, otherwise the child will have no impression of it and won't learn it.

B. Listen to level-appropriate English radio programs and tapes/CDs instead of local Chinese programs.

C. Listen to the CDs matching the English books your child uses in class (this one is so obvious, but many families don't do it).

When listening to the CD, there are some techniques which make for more effective learning:

a. Have the child point to the book with his finger following the words on the CD

This is especially important for small children who, without parental supervision, easily lose focus.

b. Have the child repeat aloud after the CD

Another method to help children keep focused, with the added long-term benefit of improving speaking skills.

c. Repeat listening to the CD (the more the better!)

The more often a language CD is listened to, the deeper impression it will make on a student. But, as mentioned above, divided practice is best. If you plan to listen three times, divide that practice over three days. The result will be bet-

出來，孩子睡覺前又可以再聽一次了！

四、和孩子一起觀賞適合其程度的電影或電視

五、帶孩子一起讀英文讀本

除了陪孩子一起複習補習班的教材之外，和孩子一起唸讀本也是一個幫忙孩子學習英文很好的方法；選購讀本時，除了本書之前有關美語補習班教材所提過的內容外，可以遵循以下這些準則：

一、適合學生程度

基本上一頁裡，學生會遇到的新單字以不超過5%為宜，否則單字太多，學生可能會失去興趣。

二、選擇有單字、句型系統的讀本爲主，故事性的讀本爲輔

現在坊間有些教材的編寫是以使用頻率最高的英文單字所寫成，並強調單字的重覆性。這樣子的教材可以做為學習的主教材，因為學生可以很快的學會一些最常用到的單字。然而，由於受到所使用的單字及句型的限制，以單字句型為主的讀本就沒有辦法像一般故事讀本來的活潑。因此，最好的做法會是以單字句型這一類的讀本做為主要教材，而以故事讀本做為輔助教材。

三、儘量選擇搭配有聲教材的教材

如果家長本身的英文能力不足時，最好選擇搭配有聲教材（錄音帶、CD、VCD、DVD等）的讀本。對於初學者而言，市面上有些教材的有聲教材是以中、英雙語錄製而成的，亦是不錯的選擇。

六、在家中儘量和孩子用英文互動－－不要害怕會犯錯要和孩子一起學習

孩子口說能力如果要好，光靠一周二次到補習班去上課的時間是不夠

ter than trying to listen three times at one sitting.

A further note: children don't have to quietly sit at a table when listening to a CD. Instead, think creatively of opportunities to make use of time. For example, one of our students puts on the CD when he goes to bed. There are always a few minutes before we fall asleep, so we can use a language CD to both review and lull us to sleep. Some other times? On waking up, brushing teeth, playing with toys, sitting in the car, drawing a picture, and the list goes on.

D. Watch English TV and movies, especially ones appropriate to their language level.

E. Read English storybooks together.

Separate from reviewing English class curriculum, reading enjoyable storybooks is an excellent method to help children learn English. When choosing storybooks, apart from previously mentioned notes on class curriculum, consider the following criteria:

a. Find stories at the appropriate language level

A simple rule of thumb would be fewer than 5% of words counted as new vocabulary; otherwise, if there are too many new words, children will lose interest

b. Choose books that focus on systematic use of vocabulary And sentence structures and which also employ an enjoyable storytelling format.

Many booksellers now carry works which focus on repetitive use of the most frequently used English vocabulary. These books can function as a basic curriculum, allowing students to quickly learn the most common language forms. However, because of limits on vocabulary and sentence structure, these "readers" are generally unable to equal the enjoyably active nature of storybooks. Therefore, it might be best to use "readers" as a core curriculum with storybooks

的。因此，如果有機會，儘量用英文和孩子做互動是很重要的。但大部份家長可能會擔心自己英文能力不足，而有不敢和孩子做練習這樣子的迷思，其實大可不必。如果孩子發現家長也和自己一起學習，這不也是一種很好的身教嗎？而且，不見得一定是要家長教、孩子學，如果孩子學得不錯，讓孩子來教你也是一個好方法。或者是遇到問題時，家長和孩子一起查書、查字典找出問題的答案，有些學生家長是採用這樣子的方式，效果也都不錯。如果家長更用心一點，和孩子一起學習他們補習班的英文教材，這樣子良性的互動不但可以讓孩子的英文能力大大的提升，更可為親子關係加溫！

很多家長不敢自己教孩子英文的另一個原因是他們覺得自己的英文發音不好，他們希望可以讓孩子學習「正統英文發音」。每次有家長這樣子說時，我都會問他們：「你所謂正統的英文發音是指哪一種？」他們往往口答：「就是外國人的發音啊！」全世界說英文的國家為數眾多，美國、英國、南非、澳洲......每個國家的腔調都不一樣，英文發音其實沒有所謂正不正統。且學英文最主要的目的在於溝通，就像聯合國開會時，雖然大家說英文的腔調都不太一樣，可是溝通的目的達到了才是重點。在台灣也有許多英文學好得很的人，以他們自己的「台灣腔」為榮；因為英文本來就不是我們的母語，大可不必花太多的時間在學習外國人講話的腔調。發音要求正確度，而不是求「正統」。

如果怕自己的發音可能不正確，電子字典是個很不錯的學習用具。現在市面上有些電子字典的發音已經做到和真人發音很像了，這對於還不懂K.K.音標的孩子，或者是想和孩子一起學英文的家長來說都是一樣很好的工具。

employed in a supporting role.

c. Strive to choose curriculum that has matching audio material

Many parents realize their limited English ability, so it's best to find books which include audio aids (CD, VCD, CD-ROM). This can be especially beneficial to beginning learners. There are abundant audio and bilingual materials on the market today.

F. Try to use English at home as much as possible

Don't be afraid to make mistakes! Laugh and learn together. If children are to develop good verbal skills, attending a twice-a-week class is not enough. Therefore, it is important to use English at home whenever possible. Most parents feel their own English is insufficient and may be afraid to practice with their children. This is unnecessary and counterproductive. When children find parents want to study with them, this acts as a form of learning by example. Additionally, is it necessary always for the parents to teach and the children to learn? Can we not sometimes turn the table and, when children learn well, allow them to teach us, the parents? When facing a problem, parent and child can together look for the answer, check the dictionary and find the answer. Some of our student families use this method to great effect. If parents actively learn with children, the result will be not only better English for both child and parent, but a warmer family relationship.

Poor pronunciation is another reason parents hesitate to teach their children English. Naturally, they wish for children to learn "correct pronunciation." Every time a parent brings up this question, I ask, "Which English pronunciation do you regard as correct?" As expected, they answer, "Foreigners' pronunciation!" In all the world, there are many countries for which English is the national or mother tongue. A short list would include the United States, Canada,

七、剛學過的單字要不斷的重複強調

把最近學過的20個字，列一張表，並經常地使用他們。

如果家長可以努力落實以上這七個要點，學生即使沒有辦法在一個全美語的環境下學習，他們的學習效果也還是可以達到相當的水準！重點就在於父母是不是真得付出心力幫孩子營造一個更好的英文學習環境！

England, Ireland, Scotland, Australia, and New Zealand, but there are many more. And each of those nations has a different "English" pronunciation. In fact, inside of each nation there is a wide variety of different pronunciations. In the United States, a person from Texas, a person from California, a person from Ohio, and a person from New York will all speak differently. So what is "correct?" No one standard exists. The goal of learning English is for communication. Just as in the United Nations, though everyone speaks English differently, the goal of communication is met and that's what is important. People in Taiwan can learn English well and need not be embarrassed about speaking with a Taiwan accent, and they need not spend gobs of time pursuing a foreign accent. Speaking in a clear understandable way does not mean chasing a false or impossible "standard."

If you are still afraid your pronunciation is not good enough, there are on the market some electronic dictionaries which are able to closely mimic the quality of real human voices. This is also a good option for children who have not yet mastered phonetic symbols used in dictionaries (such as K.K.).

G. Always try to focus on the vocabulary presently being learned

Make a list of the most recent 20 words and use those regularly.

If parents can actively implement the above seven suggestions, even though students have no opportunity to live in an English immersion environment, they can still achieve a relatively high level. The critical point is whether parents are willing to invest the effort to create a better learning atmosphere.

帶孩子唸讀本的步驟

閱讀之前

請孩子回想上一次所上過的內容為何；可以把課文內容遮住，只給孩子看圖片，問：〝What happened last time？〞請孩子試著用英文告訴你上次上過的內容。

1. 用之前學過的單字、句型來問他們問題：問題的型態基本上就是用「6個w」（what, who, when, why, where ,how）, do/does, is/am/are,及can這些疑問字來提問題。
2. 看圖回答問題：在讀新的內容之前，問孩子： "What can you see in the picture？"或提問和圖片有關的問題。

開始閱讀

一. 講解新的單字: 講解新單字時主要的方法有二個

1. 直接用中文翻譯：這是最省時的方法，且遇到較籠統的概念（如解釋before、after）時比較容易解釋清楚。
2. 用英文解釋：如果家長本身的英文能力不錯，且孩子學習英文也有一段時間後可以使用。解釋時不需用很難的單字，事實上，用較簡單的英文單字或者是動作，往往就可以解釋得很清楚了。例如解釋〝cry〞時，字典上的定義是"to produce tears from the eyes as a sign of sorrow"，這樣子的解釋孩子是不可能聽得懂的。如把用字簡化一下成"cry is something a baby does when he/she is hungry"，或者直接做出哭的動作，孩子自然馬上就理解了。

Steps in leading children to read

Pre-reading

a. Reflect: guide children to reflect on the content and vocabulary of the last lesson. One simple method is to look at text illustrations and ask the following (with the child answering in English), "What happened last time? What is this about? How do you say that word?"

b. Use previous vocabulary and sentence patterns to ask the child questions. Focus on the "6 Ws" (what, who, when, why, where, how), which elicit more complete answers. The "yes/no" questions (do/does, am/is/are, can, will) may be used to supplement.

c. Before reading new text, look at the illustrations and ask, "What can you see in this picture? What do you think they are doing? Why are they doing that?" or other questions regarding the content.

During Reading

A. Two important methods to use when explaining new vocabulary

a. Directly translate Using Chinese: this is the quickest method, and when dealing with general concepts (like "before, after") will usually lead to a clearer understanding.

b. Use English to explain: useful if the parent's English ability is sufficient and the child has some foundation. There is no need to use difficult words to explain. In fact, the goal is to explain things simply, in a way the child will understand using words or actions that are easily understood. For example, where the dictionary might define "cry" as "to produce tears form the eyes as a sign of sorrow" (what kid learning English

3. 折衷法：也就是在孩子可以理解的範圍內儘量使用英文，再穿插中文的解釋，這樣孩子學習的效果會最好。

二. 孩子閱讀

請孩子自己讀，如果有不會唸的單字，或發音有錯誤時，家長再與予協助。

三. 孩子用中文解釋句子的意思

以確定孩子了解課文及單字的內容。

四. 每一頁讀完的後續活動

1. 家長問有關課文的內容，孩子回答。
2. 學生當老師：學習一段時間之後可以讓學生來當老師問你問題。
3. 回想：把課本闔上，請孩子用英文告訴你剛唸完那一頁的大概內容為何。

閱讀之後

1. 聽讀本的CD：以剛才提到的方式聽CD。
2. 新的單字：對於年紀比較小的孩子，新的單字可以請他們抄寫5至10遍以加深印象；如果孩子年紀較大或吸收能力較好時，則可以讓孩子背單字（但之後還是要持續的複習，以確定孩子是真正的學會了）。

要特別注意的是儘量把上課學到的句子融入真實情境中，舉例來說，如果學生今天在讀本裡學到了「like to+動詞」這個句型，則家長就可以問孩子"What do you like to do？"或"Do you like to eat ice cream？"或是請他們做中翻英（例如請孩子告訴你「我喜歡吃冰淇淋」這個句子英文怎麼說）。學過一個句型後，儘量用在和孩子日常的互動中，這樣孩子印象當然也就特別深刻了！

would understand that?), you could either simplify this with "cry is something a baby does when he/she is hungry," or simply act it out by crying—instant understanding!

c. Compromise: use English as much as possible within a child's vocabulary limitations, then where necessary explain in Chinese. This will lead to the best results.

B. The child reads: ask the child to read, and only help when the child encounters a word he cannot read correctly.

C. The child explains the meaning of a sentence or passage in Chinese: this is to ensure understanding of both individual words and content.

D. Follow-up activities after reading a page:

a. The parent asks pertinent questions about the content.

b. Reverse roles (student becomes teacher): after reading for a period, the child asks the parent questions.

c. Reflect: cover the book and ask the child to use English to paraphrase what was just read.

Post Reading

1. Listen to the accompanying CD: use the methods mentioned above.
2. New words: for younger children, have them write down the words 5 to 10 times to deepen their impression. For older children or those who learn faster, ask them to memorize the words (but always go back later to check memory).

Special attention should be paid to use vocabulary and sentence patterns in realistic situations. For example, if the child today read the pattern "like to + verb" the parent could ask, "What do you like to do?" or "Do you like to eat ice cream?" Another method is for the parent to provide the Chinese equivalent ("Do you like to eat ice cream?") and ask the child to produce the English. Once a

和孩子一起學習

如果你告訴孩子，學習英文是一件很重要的事時，你一定要記得以下這個原則：身教大於言教。你是否願意和孩子一起坐下來讀英文、聽CD，並一起練習呢？我每天都會抽出一點時間和我的女兒們讀英文，我的做法是要他們唸英文書給我聽，我糾正他們的發音，我還會再問一些問題以確定他們了解課文及某些特定單字的意思。這是一個帶孩子唸英文很好的方法，而且這樣一來，不只是你的孩子，連你也跟著在學習了。

讓孩子了解學習是很重要的

我已經數不清告訴過女兒多少次，學習英文的重要性。如果你能不斷的強調某樣東西的重要性，你的孩子會比較容易也有同樣的看法。

想想以下這一個例子：如果你的小孩數學成績很差，而你只是無關緊要的說：「下次再努力一點就好啦！」長久下來，你覺得你的孩子還會認為數學是一門對他日後學習上扮演重要角色的科目嗎？

真正發生的狀況是，孩子會因著你長期以來對某件事的看法而改變他自己的看法。如果今天你告訴你的孩子學習英文是很重要的，可是隔一天你卻又表現出英文並不是很重要的態度，孩子會將你的行為解讀成「爸媽說一套、做一套」或「很困惑，乾脆放棄好了」。在生活中，處理孩子問題的前後標準要一致，學習外語當然也是一樣的。

因此，我鼓勵家長坐下來，和孩子談談為什麼學習英文很重要，舉例子讓他們可以更清楚的了解，並且用一貫的態度來處理相關學習上的問題。

sentence pattern is established, strive to then use that in daily conversation with the child. Naturally, the child's impression will deepen greatly. With repeated use over time, language learning success is virtually guaranteed!

Sit with the child and practice together

You tell your child English is important, but remember this rule: actions speak louder than words. Are you willing to sit with your child, read through the books, listen to the CDs, and practice together? I try to make time every day to sit with my daughters and read English. I have them read while I listen for correct pronunciation, and then I ask questions to make sure they understand both the general content and specific words. This is an excellent way to spend time together with your children and engage in an activity that will help both you and them.

Help the child understand learning is very important

I cannot count the number of times I have told my daughters and explained to them about the value of learning English. When a child understands that something is very important, and that you, the parent regard it as imperative, then he or she is much more likely to consider it important, too.

Think about this example. If your child were doing very poorly at school in math, came home with a low test score, and you just shrugged, saying, "Try harder next time," do you think that child would grow to regard math as something important to learn, something integral to his academic future?

孩子表現得好時要給予鼓勵

當然每一個家庭都有自己的一套獎懲方式，而且也沒有任何一種獎懲方式是放諸四海而皆準的。不過，基本上可以遵循以下這兩個大原則：

要訂定一套表現良好時的獎勵辦法

我還清楚的記得在我很小的時候，我的父母告訴我們幾個兄弟，如果我們的學期成績可以全部拿A，除了得到美金5塊錢之外，還有權決定全家人到哪一家餐廳去吃飯。

五塊錢聽起來好像不是很多，可是當我還是小學三年級、四年級的時候，五塊錢感覺上是很大的一筆數目，而且能決定全家人到哪一家餐廳去吃飯是一件很光榮的事。對我而言，這是一個很好的鼓勵方式，這也讓我在求學的路上付出更多心力在學習上。事實上，一直到大學，我每一次都達到父母的這個要求！

找出你孩子喜歡的東西為何，並把他化為一種表現好的獎勵。曾經有一陣子，我的小女兒不想讀她的英文書。我知道她喜歡吃洋芋片，我告訴她：「每讀完一頁，我就給妳一片洋芋片。」

之後我們就一起坐在一罐洋芋片前面。我的女兒可以看到那罐洋芋片，而且她想要吃，同時她也知道如果她不讀她的英文書，她就不能得到洋芋片。結果呢？她讀了不只一頁。

良好的表現需持續的被鼓勵

我們每天要處理的事情太多、太煩雜了，有時我們會變得沮喪、疲倦和健忘；我當然也會如此。可是，我們的孩子卻是很少忘記我們對他們的承

Most often, a child will read your long-term attitude and respond to that. If today you say English is important, but tomorrow act like it doesn't really matter, the child will either understand your attitude as "say one thing but do another," or will be confused and give up. In all areas of life, consistency with our children is important, and no less so in learning a foreign language.

Therefore, I encourage parents to sit down with their children, explain clearly why English is essential in today's world, give some simple examples to help them understand, and then act in a consistent way.

Reward the child for doing well

Every family has its own way to handle reward and punishment. There is no single way, but I offer two "rules" here for your consideration:

There should be some system of reward for achievement

It's strange what we remember, but one thing I recall clearly when I was a kid is that my parents promised my brothers and me that if we achieved straight A's in school on the semester report card, we would get $5 and could choose a restaurant at which to have dinner.

Today, $5 doesn't sound like much, but when I was in 3rd and 4th grade, that seemed like a pretty big sum, and the prestige of choosing any restaurant to have dinner with my parents was a big plus. For me, this was a great encouragement and I'm sure it helped boost my performance for many years. In fact, I held my parents to their promise all the way through college!

Find something your kids value and turn that into an achievement award. For a while, my younger daughter didn't want to read her English book, but I knew she liked eating potato chips. I told her, "One page equals one potato chip." Then we sat down with the book and I put the can of chips in front of us. She

諾。如果我們答應他們的獎勵，卻沒有做到，他們為把這件事看成是虛偽或是拒絕。我們必需對他們的需求非常敏感，並且必須不斷的獎勵他們。因此，我建議家長選擇孩子可以真正覺得被鼓勵到的獎勵方式，並且要時時的給孩子獎勵。例如，給年紀夠大的孩子少量的零用錢做為獎勵。我記得我以前讀過一本書，書中一位父親答應每次他女兒讀完一本書後就給她一塊錢，而他女兒最後讀完書的數量幾乎和一間小型圖書館的藏書一樣多。這個主意聽起來很不錯，所以我對我的女兒們也用同樣的方法。

 孩子表現不好時的處罰方式

聖經上有一段關於如何教導小孩的經節，而這條經文幾千年來已教導了無數的父母；這段經文就是箴言23章12節「要認真管教兒童」，而這也就是我們時常講的「孩子不打不成器」的道理。

懲罰有許多不同的方式，不見得一定要體罰。對於我自己的小孩，如果他們不是故意違背我的規定，我是不會用體罰的方式的。

另一個較簡單的懲罰小孩的方式是不給他們想要的東西。舉例來說，如果我規定我女兒寫一頁英文作業而她卻沒有做，我可能會說：「妳今天晚上不準看電視」；或者如果兩個女兒一個寫了作業而另一個沒有，我會帶字作業的那一個出去吃冰淇淋。

另外，規定孩子完成某件事所用的語言要儘量的明確，因為如果沒有很清楚的準則，往往就會產生誤會。舉例來說，當我告訴我的女兒：「去讀書！」，也許她的確拿起書來看了，但我們兩個人對她該讀到哪一個程度可能會有認知上的落差。我可能覺得她應該要複習先前學過的五頁，讀兩頁新的，並標出所有她不懂的單字。可是，我如果沒有很清楚的規定她該讀的進

could see the chips, and she wanted them, but she knew if she didn't read, she couldn't eat them. Guess what? She didn't want to read just one page.

Achievement should be rewarded consistently

There are so many things every day that clutter our lives, sometimes we get frustrated, frazzled, and forgetful. I certainly do. However, our children rarely forget the promises we make to them. If we offer a reward and don't come through, they'll see it either as hypocrisy or rejection. We need to be sensitive to their needs. We need to reward consistently. So I suggest choosing rewards that are both prized by them and which we can give regularly, for example, a small amount of spending money for a child who is old enough to appreciate money. I remember reading of a father who promised to give his daughter US$1 for each book she read and how that encouraged her to read a small library of books. That sounded like an excellent idea, so now I do the equivalent with my daughters.

Some form of punishment for failure

Another good Bible verse that has instructed parents for thousands of years is Proverbs 23:13 "Do not withhold discipline from a child," which is commonly known as "Spare the rod and spoil the child."

Punishment comes in many forms; it does not have to be physical. For my children, I try to reserve physical punishment (spanking) only for willful acts of disobedience.

Simple forms of punishment may come in the form of withholding things the child wants. For example, if I tell my daughter to do a written page of English homework and she doesn't do it, then I may say, "No television tonight." Or perhaps if one daughter does her work but the other doesn't, I'll take the one who did out for an ice cream.

度，她可能坐下來讀一、兩頁之後就跑去玩電腦了。

這裡的重點和我們先前提到有關如何獎勵孩子大致相同，父母應該：

一、 明確的告訴孩子他們該完成的事情為何。

二、 訂定一套明確和一貫的懲罰原則。

以正面的態度來解決孩子學習不良的問題

當一個小孩的學習成效不佳時，不管原因為何，做父母的可能會有兩種反應，一種是正面的，另一種則是負面的。

第一種正面反應，同時也是較好的，就是父母會試著去找出孩子為什麼學習成效不好的原因，並對症下藥。是因為孩子沒有學習動機嗎？如果是這樣，你可能要再進一步問，該怎麼做才能讓小孩子有學習動機呢？是否需要訂定努力的目標和獎勵方式，讓孩子有努力的方向？下一個問題，也就是我們在這一章前面提到過的，就是有關於營造居家學習環境的問題。身為父母，我是不是有安排孩了每天唸英文的時間，並確定我的孩子是不是都按時的完成他該完成的作業。每天花一點時間練習對學好一種語言的重要性是再怎麼強調都不為過的。

另一種反應是負面的。我曾遇過一些家長，當他們的小孩學習成效或參加比賽成績不如預期時，他們就不讓小孩繼續到我班上上課。當然他們不見得一定要把小孩送到我的班上上課，可是，如果他們的小孩在公立學校的學習成績不好時，他們難道也要把孩子的課停掉嗎？當然不是，一般的做法應該是找出問題癥結的所在，並想辦法改善這個情形。對大多數學習成效不好

There should be a clear understanding of what is expected. Without clear guidelines, confusion will be common. For example, if I tell my daughter to "read her book" and she sits down to do so, we may have completely different ideas of what she should do. Perhaps I think she should review the last five pages and read two new pages of text, being careful to mark down new vocabulary. However, without my clearly stating these objectives, she may sit down and read one or two pages, then put the book down and go play on the computer.

The main points here are very much like those mentioned above in rewarding a child for doing well. Parents should establish:

A. a clear understanding of what is expected

B. a clear and consistent system of punishment for failure

Find positive steps to address and resolve failure

When a student is failing, whatever the reason, there are two responses from parents, one positive and the other negative.

The first response, which is good, is for the parent to search for and discover the root of the trouble and then to work toward correcting that problem. Is the student unmotivated? Then ask, what can I do to motivate my child? Does the child need a goal or prize to strive for? The next question, as explained earlier in this chapter, regards the home learning environment. As a parent, am I making sure my child practices English on a regular basis, just as I make sure my child does his/her school homework? I cannot overemphasize how important daily practice is to learning a language.

The second response is negative. I have had parents who, when their child does poorly or not as well as they want in some test or competition, removed

的學生而言，這就意謂著他們必須要花更多時間、更勤快的練習。

很奇怪的是，就學習英文這一件事而言，許多父母很不重視小孩本身須更勤快練習的這一部份。每次班上有學習成效不太好的學生時，我一定先問他的父母：「他在家有沒有每天練習？」十個裡面有九個的答案是：「沒有」，而且父母往往會給一堆藉口解釋為什麼他的小孩沒有辦法每天練習。

這和我先前提到有關父母跟孩子強調學習英文的重要性有相呼應，如果父母沒有要求小孩子練習，小孩很自然的就會以為學習英文不是很重要的事。如果學英文並不是很重要，那為什麼還要花時間學習呢？對於年紀較小的學生而言，我深信學習的責任和練習都有賴於父母。而當學生年紀較大了之後，這個練習的責任才會慢慢轉移到他們自己的身上。

可是如果一位學生在家裡已經花時間練習，但學習成效卻還是不好時該怎麼辦呢？很多時候，如果一個小孩在家裡有複習，那可能就要看他練習的方法到底對不對了。如果有複習還是學不好時，這個小孩如果不是沒有專心在學習的東西上，就是練習的方法錯了。

如果是這種情形，我建議你和學生的英文老師連絡，並討論在家裡如何更有效的幫助孩子做練習。此外，複習一下先前「英語學習簡介」這一章來看有關記憶和練習方法的重點。

我深信，如果採用正確的教材和教學法，再加上父母的鼓勵，每個小孩的英文都可以學得很好的。

their child from class. Of course, they don't have to come to my class. But do they remove their child from public school when the child does poorly on a test there? No, the usual response is to find out what's wrong and correct it. For most, that means practicing more and being more diligent in learning.

Strangely, when it comes to learning English, many parents have little interest in practice and diligence on the part of their children. Whenever I find a child is doing poorly in class, the first question I ask the parent is, "Is the student practicing regularly at home?" Probably 90% of the time, the answer is no, following which the parent invariably comes up with lots of excuses why the student isn't practicing.

This directly relates to my earlier point regarding parents teaching children the value of learning English. If the parent does not require the child to practice, then the child will implicitly understand English is not important. If English is not really important, then why bother spending time to practice and learn it? When it comes to young children, I believe the responsibility for learning and practice mostly lies with the parents. As children grow older, they take over that responsibility.

So what about the other 10% of the time? Most often, if the child is reviewing at home, it is a matter of incorrect practice. Either the child is not focused in studying and is just going through the motions, or is practicing in the wrong ways.

If this is the case, then I suggest you have a meeting with your English teacher and discuss effective methods for home practice. Also, review the previous chapter "Introduction to English Language Learning" for important notes about memory and practice.

I believe, given the right materials and methods, and properly encouraged by parents, every child can learn English well.

一些提醒事項

（一個父親給其他父母的話）

A Few Last Notes and Anecdotes (from one parent to another)

我也是一位家長。現在著手寫這本書的同時，我的兩個女兒也都在國小就讀。我很能體會父母對小孩的期望和夢想是什麼，自己也很希望兩個小孩在生命的旅程中能走得很順利，有個成功的人生。這也就是我寫這一本書的目的，同時也是我為所有父母禱告的內容，希望你們的孩子都能夠成功。

但是，「成功」的定義為何呢？你又該如何幫助您的孩子成功的學習英文這個「國際性的語言」呢？

「上帝的憐憫每日都更新」（耶利米哀歌3：23）

我相信你一定有聽過萊特兄弟，也就是飛機發明人的故事。而事實上，如果你還記得的話，萊特兄弟不過是兩個修理腳踏車的工人罷了。但有另一個故事你可能不知道，那就是在萊特兄弟的時代，有一位很聰明的科學家寫了很多關於飛行的著作，他就是南利博士（Dr. Samuel P. Langley），當時大家都覺得他應該會比萊特兄弟早成功。

可是後來南利博士到哪去了呢？當南利博士第一次試驗飛行時，他沒有成功。事實上，他的飛機墜毀了，而當時的新聞媒體稱這個事件為「荒謬的慘敗」。

南利博士是不是就此放棄了呢？不，他並沒有理會外界的批評而繼續在他的研究上努力。兩個月後，他又試飛了一次，這一次飛機栽到了河裡，飛行員差點淹死。約紐時報稱這個事件是「南利的愚蠢行為」，並認為他應該要放棄他的計畫。

南利博士是否能不在乎別人的看法，繼續專心在他的研究上呢？不幸的是，他沒有；這一次他聽從了別人所說的。連續面臨了二次失敗後，他放棄了他一生的夢想，而也因而未能看到他自己設計的飛機在天空飛翔。

九天之後，沒有受過高等教育且沒有別人贊助的萊特兄弟將他們的飛機－－飛行者一號－－送上天際，也從此在歷史上留名青史。諷刺的是，當萊

I am a parent. As I write this, I have two daughters in elementary school. I know what it is for parents to have hopes and dreams for their children. I very much want for my children to grow, develop, and succeed in their lives. That's why my goal in writing this book for you, and my prayer for you as parents, is for your children to succeed.

But what does "success" mean? And how can you help your children to succeed in learning English, the "world language"?

I began this book with a quote from the Bible. Let me add another here, in the concluding chapter.

"God's mercies begin afresh each day." Lamentations 3:23

I'm sure you've heard of the Wright brothers, who pioneered the first airplane. You may recall they were, in fact, just two bicycle mechanics. But what you probably don't know is that at the same period of time there was a brilliant scientist who'd written volumes on the subject of flight. He was Dr. Samuel P. Langley, and he was expected to succeed in flight before the Wright brothers.

So what happened to Langley? Well, when Langley tried to fly his first plane, it didn't work as planned. In fact, it crashed and the press labeled it "a ridiculous fiasco."

Did Langley give up? No, he ignored their criticism and stayed focused. Two months later, when he tried again, the plane plunged upside down into a river and the pilot almost drowned. This time the New York Times labeled it "Langley's Folly" and said he should give up.

Did Langley ignore their criticism and go back to the drawing board? Unfortunately, no. This time he listened. Facing failure and criticism a second time, he gave up his life's dream without ever seeing one of his planes in the air.

Nine days later, Orville and Wilbur Wright, with no education and no funds,

特兄弟變成家喻戶曉的人物時，南利早就被人們所遺忘了。

從這個故事中我們學到了什麼？南利為什麼失敗？

首先，他認為一時的失敗和別人給他的羞辱就如同世界末日一般；這也正是他的致命傷。他可能認為一時的失敗就代表著未來再也沒有成功的機會了。

其次，他沒有辦法看到在失敗的背後，成功就在不遠的前方。

當我們成功的時候，其他的一切事情似乎都不再重要了；突然之間我們覺得我們可以征服任何事。當然，我們也都知道這樣子的感覺不會持續很久。

當我們身處困境時我們也會有同樣的感覺。當遇上災難時，我們可能會覺得這就是世界末日；突然之間，我們覺得我們沒有辦法做好任何事，覺得自己是「失敗者」。

這兩種感覺都是不實際的。成功沒有辦法讓我們成為超人，就好像失敗不會要了我們的命一樣。

你可能覺得很奇怪，這和學英文到底又有什麼關係呢？

關於失敗，讓我們再來看看上一章最後我提到一些英文學習成效不太好的學生。當一個學生學習成效不好時，最好停下來想一想到底問題出在哪？如果你已經嚴格選擇美語補習班、老師和教材，而孩子卻還是學不好，這時，如果不是孩子沒有學習動機，那可能就是居家學習的環境出了問題。另外一個可能是，你是不是對孩子的要求太高了？就像希望女兒們在各方面都能成為佼佼者，但他們不可能達到這個目標，世界上也沒有任何人可以，因為那不是人所能達到的境界。

失敗了999次才成功的發明電燈泡，我們是不是該慶幸他在失敗了第100次時沒有決定放棄。愛因斯坦的老師認為他有學習障礙，是個智障。慶

flew their plane, Flyer One, over the sands of Kittyhawk and into the history books. Sadly, while most of the world today has heard of the Wright Brothers, Langley is almost unknown.

So, what's the lesson to be learned? Why did Langley fail?

First, he considered his failure and public humiliation to be the end, a mortal wound. He probably decided that the momentary disappointment and loss meant no possibility for future triumph.

Second, he couldn't see beyond his failure to the success that was waiting just around the corner.

In a moment of triumph, we feel that nothing else really matters. We feel suddenly like we can conquer anything. Of course, we all know that doesn't last long.

The reverse is also true. When we are caught in a moment of disaster, we feel like that's the end of everything. Suddenly, we can't succeed at anything. We are "losers".

Neither feeling is realistic. Success doesn't turn us into supermen, just as failure doesn't have to be fatal.

So now you're wondering, what does this have to do with learning English?

Regarding failure, let me first remind you of the notes in the last chapter regarding students of mine who haven't done well in learning English. When a student doesn't do well, it is best to first think carefully about why this happens. If you have looked carefully for a superior school with good teachers, materials and methods, then failure usually means either a lack of motivation on the part of the student or a lack of home learning environment. A final problem could be this: are your expectations too high? As much as I want my daughters to always be first in whatever they do, they won't be. No one can. It is not human.

Yes, set high goals. Look for high standards. But failure is often the next

幸的是，他不在意他們的看法，後來成為當時最有名的科學家。

如果你的小孩學習成效不是很好，試著找出問題的所在，並對症下藥。問題和錯誤往往都是學習成長的好機會；而也因為失敗，我們才可以邁向成功之路。

 雙語恐懼感

有些父母認為孩子沒有辦法同時學好兩種語言；也有一些父母用帶著質疑的心態以訛傳訛的說：「小孩子如果國語還沒學好，就不應該學英語！」。他們擔心英文會混淆孩子學習國語的能力。

讓我向你保證，情形不是這樣子的。如果方法正確，不要說兩種，小孩子可以同時學會三種、甚至四種以上的語言！讓我以我自身的經驗來驗證這個說法。

我的一個好朋友在南斯拉夫長大，她的父母來自匈牙利，所以她從小就學會說匈牙利語和塞爾維亞一克羅地亞語，她並在六歲時開始學英語（也就是她所學的第三種語言）。當我們成為朋友時，她的英文已經達到幾乎如母語般的流利程度了。也就是說，他可以很流利的說三種語言，而這些語言都是她從很小的時候就開始學習。

我的女兒們是另一個好的例子；基本上，國語才是她們的母語。我太太在家和她們說國語，而由於她們在台灣長大，他們的學校老師、朋友、電視、廣播等等創造出了一個全中文的環境。我在我的女兒四歲時開始教她們英文。讓很多美國人驚訝的是，他們的英文既流利又道地，就像美國小孩一樣。

早期的雙語教育有影響他們學習中文的能力嗎？這我留給你自己來判

step toward success. It is said that Thomas Edison failed 999 times in his quest to make a light bulb. Aren't we glad he didn't stop after failure number 100? It is also said that Einstein's schoolteachers thought he was a "slow" student, intellectually impaired. Thankfully, he didn't listen to them but went on to become the most famous scientist of his time.

If your child isn't doing well, find out what's wrong and fix it. Problems and mistakes are often opportunities to learn and grow. Through failure we can learn the road to success.

The Bilingual Fear

Some parents are apprehensive that children may not be able to learn two languages at once. A number of parents, either in the form of a question or a statement, have passed on this rumor: "A young child who has not yet mastered Mandarin should not begin learning English," for fear that the English will confuse the child and interfere with his ability to learn Mandarin well.

Let me assure you, this is not the case. If properly taught, a young child can learn not just two but three or even four languages. Allow me to illustrate from my personal experience.

A good friend of mine grew up in Yugoslavia. Her parents were from Hungary, so as a child she grew up speaking both Hungarian and Serbo-Croatian. She began formally learning English (therefore, her third language) at age 6, and when we became friends her English was already at near-native level. In other words, she was fluent in three languages, all started when she was a young child.

My daughters are another good example. In essence, Mandarin is their native language. Their mother speaks Mandarin with them at home, and growing up in

斷！以現在寫作的時間而言，我大女兒是國小六年級，她在學校國語考試成績幾乎都是在96到100分之間，而學校老師還選她代表學校參加縣內的國語演講比賽，她更得到了第二名。

請放心，孩子很小就學習多種語言並不會有任何不良影響。事實上，如果方法得宜，你的孩子反而會佔很大的優勢，尤其是當他們學的是像英文這樣子國際性的語言。

讓我給你一個最近發生的例子。一個禮拜前，我遇到以前的一位學生。他現在在國內一所數一數二的國立大學就讀，他從很小就跟我一起學英文，一直持續到高中畢業（中間他有停頓了一些時間）。他告訴我，在他所讀的大學中，學生如果想要修習某些特定科目的話，他們大學聯考的英文成績必須要很高（九十分以上）。此外，他還告訴我，他們學校有些課是外籍老師用全英文上課的。因為他曾和我學了很長一段時間，我知道他的英文很好，所以我問他，他們班上同學是如何也把英文學得這麼好，他的答案讓我非常驚訝：「我們班上其他學生都在國外住過或讀過書。」

這讓我覺得非常不可思議！我問他說這怎麼可能！他說他同學的父母全都是國際貿易從業人員、外交官或駐外人員。

現在你應該就明白我上面所提「如果方法得宜，你的孩子會佔很大的優勢」這一句話的涵義了吧？我的這個學生在年紀很小時就開始學習英文；因此，即使他沒有到國外去讀過書，他在一個英文的環境中還是有辦法和一些所謂「有國際背景」的學生來競爭。

不要耽誤你的小孩，因為從小就學習兩種以上的語言這件事本身並沒有錯。事實上，如果採用的方法得當，你將為你的小孩開啟未來更多的可能。

Taiwan, their schoolteachers, friends, television, radio, and others create a Mandarin environment. I began teaching both of my daughters English at age four. Yet, many Americans have remarked with surprise that their English is fluent and native, the same as any American child.

Has this early bilingualism hurt their Mandarin abilities? I'll let you be the judge. At the date of this writing, my older daughter is in sixth grade. On her school Mandarin language tests she regularly scores from 96 to 100, and the school teachers chose her to represent them in a countywide Mandarin speaking contest, at which she placed second.

Please rest assured there is nothing wrong with learning more than one language at an early age. In fact, if done properly, your child will be at a distinct advantage to other children, especially if your child is learning a world language like English.

Let me give you a very recent example. Just a week ago, I met one of my previous students. He's now studying at a top-tier university, but he began learning English with me at a fairly young age, and he continued through (with a few breaks) until his high school graduation. During our conversation, he revealed that, in order to be admitted to his college class, all the students had to score extremely high (over 90) in the entrance English test. In addition, he told me he has several foreigners teaching classes all in English. Since he had studied with me for a long time, I knew his English was good, so I asked how his classmates had learned English so well. Then he revealed the following surprise:

"Every single one of the other students has lived and studied overseas."

I was astonished at this! I asked how that was possible. He said the parents of all these students are mostly international businessmen or government diplomats, like ambassadors, who are stationed overseas.

 健康的身體有助於學習

這裡有一些心得我想分享，希望你可以有耐心把它唸完。有些事，人們可能會忽視或覺得無關緊要；然而，除了我個人深信之外，很多的科學證據也證明了下列這些因素，會對我們的學習、健康和整體身心健全有很大的影響。

睡眠

我曾有和我太太討論過小孩子的睡眠問題。我想大多數人都清楚知道，睡眠是很重要的，可是我知道有一些學生剝奪了他們自己的睡眠時間，因為他們認為花時間唸書才是比較重要的。事實上，一夜好眠可以讓學習的效果更好。一個睡眠時間不足的學生上課會沒有辦法專心，且其解決問題的能力也會減低。如果你需要一些科學的證據，以下是三則最近的報告。

Now do you see why I wrote above, "if done properly, your child will be at a distinct advantage to other children"? This student of mine began learning English early. As a result, although he has never lived or studied overseas, he is able to compete in an English environment with "international" students.

Don't hamper your child. There is nothing wrong with learning more than one language at an early age. By doing so with a proper method, you will actually free your child and open doors to an exciting array of future possibilities.

Good Health Facilitates Learning

There are some other notes I would like to share with you, if you have the patience to keep reading. These are aspects many people overlook or consider unimportant. However, I believe, and there is scientific evidence to prove, that these factors greatly affect learning, health, and our general well being.

Sleep

One topic I've discussed with my wife regards our children's sleep. It should go without saying that sleep is important, but I know many students who deprive themselves of sleep because they think it is better to spend more time studying. In fact, a good night's sleep helps us to study better. A student who is sleep-deprived will have difficulty concentrating in class and solving problems. If you need scientific evidence, here are reports from three recent studies：

2003年11月8號，聯合媒體(the Associated Press)的報告指出：「最近的一個發現顯示，媽媽說晚上要好好睡覺這個觀念是對的；科學家發現良好的睡眠對記憶力有很正面的影響」。執行這個實驗的科學家指出這結果可能會影響學生的學習習慣。芝加哥大學神經生物學Daniel Margoliash教授指出：「我想我們都有過這一種經驗，那就是睡覺前還想著一個問題該如何解決，而睡醒了之後就想到方法了。」Margoliash教授表示，其原因可能是每個人一天所要記憶的東西太多了，而有些細節在這樣子混亂的狀況下就遺失了，而睡眠時大腦能夠再一次的組織所有的記憶內容。加州大學Irvine分校的學習及記憶神經生物學中心主任James L. McGaugh表示這就像是學習另一種新的語言一樣，「這些都是關於學習對記憶的影響所做相當有趣的發現」。研究人員發現，睡得好的人在同一個測驗所得到的成績會比睡不好的人高出百分之十九。研究人員找到的證據顯示，人們的記憶要經歷過像把資料儲存在電腦的三個階段，而其中的第二階段需要睡眠。哈佛大學的研究團隊更發現，好的睡眠對隔天的表現會有很正面的影響。

On October 8, 2003, the Associated Press reported: "In a finding that backs up motherly advice to get a good night's sleep, scientists have found that peaceful slumber apparently restores memories." Researchers who conducted the experiments said the results may influence how students learn. "We all have the experience of going to sleep with a question and waking up with the solution," said Daniel Margoliash, a professor of neurobiology at the University of Chicago. Margoliash said it could be that a person acquires so many memories each day that some details are lost in that jumble, but that the brain sorts and reorganizes the memories during sleep. James L. McGaugh, director of the Center for the Neurobiology of Learning and Memory, at the University of California at Irvine, said (it) is similar to learning a new language. "These are highly interesting findings that add additional information concerning the affects of sleep on memory." The researchers found that the people who had a night's sleep had a 19 percentage point improvement over their pre-training test. The researchers found evidence that memories are consolidated in three stages in a process similar to storing data on a computer's hard drive. The second stage requires sleep, which the Harvard team also found sharpened the subject's performance the next day.

2004年1月21日，德國的一群科學家指出，他們首次發現人類的大腦在睡眠時，仍會不斷的想解決睡前所解決不了的問題。且在睡了八個小時之後，解決的方法會比較容易被想出來。德國科學家的這一個實驗被認為是史上第一個支持「創造力、解決問題和良好的睡眠」有很直接相關的證據。其他的研究者則指出，這樣子的結果對超時工作的人和學生而言做了最好的提醒；那就是睡眠通常會是問題最好的解藥。先前的研究也已經顯示，**睡眠的剝奪**和意外發生率的增加、健康的惡化及**考試成績低落都有很直接的關係**。

國家健康研究院睡眠問題研究中心主任Carl E. Hunt博士指出，這樣子的研究結果，對想要在學校及工作場所表現好的學生和工作者而言，都會有很重大的影響。

德國Luebeck大學的科學家發現，參加一項簡單數學測驗的受試者中，前一晚有睡足八個小時的受試者所解出問題的比率，是沒有睡足八小時受試者的三倍。

這項研究的領導者Jan Born指出，這樣子的結果支持生物化學的研究，認為記憶在被儲存之前都是先經過重組的。他同時表示，創造力在睡覺的過程中也會被增強。

Born表示，大腦如何增強這些能力的過程還不是很清楚，但這樣子的研究結果應該被視為是所有學校、公司老闆及政府部門的一個警訊，那就是，足夠的睡眠在心理層面的表現會有很大的影響。

Reported January 21, 2004: German scientists say they have demonstrated for the first time that our sleeping brains continue working on problems that baffle us during the day, and the right answer may come more easily after eight hours of rest. The German study is considered to be the first hard evidence supporting the common sense notion that creativity and problem solving appear to be directly linked to adequate sleep. Other researchers say it provides a valuable reminder for overtired workers and students that sleep is often the best medicine. Previous studies have shown that **sleep-deprivation contributes to** increased accidents, worsening health and **lower test scores.**

Dr. Carl E. Hunt, director of the National Center on Sleep Disorders Research at the National Institutes of Health, said this study is "going to have potentially important results for children for school performance and for adults for work performance."

Scientists at the University of Luebeck in Germany found that volunteers taking a simple math test were three times more likely than sleep-deprived participants to figure out a hidden rule for converting the numbers into the right answer if they had eight hours of sleep.

Jan Born, who led the study, said the results support biochemical studies of the brain that indicate memories are restructured before they are stored. Creativity also appears to be enhanced in the process, he said.

另一個研究也指出：「當睡眠被剝奪時，流到大腦的血液會減少百分之七到八。這除了對一個人的判斷力和記憶力會帶來不良的影響之外，也同時可能造成妄想症、憂鬱症、免疫系統功能失調，及因為內分泌失調所帶來的肥胖。」

因為這個原因，在我家裡，小孩子九點到九點半之間就要上床睡覺；隔天我們早上6:40起床，上學前上20到30分鐘讀英文。因為他們晚上睡眠的時間很長，早上他們的精神就很好，也準備好要學習了。除此之外，這樣子的做法可以確保他們每天都練習到英文。

營養

首先，我必須告訴你，我並不是一位營養師。但多年來，我一直對營養方面的議題相當有興趣（大學時我曾修課，並認真的學習營養方面的知識），且我一生都對運動相當熱衷。除此之外，如果有閱讀飲食方面報告的習慣，你會發現專業的營養師和研究者通常在觀念上會有很大的出入，甚至是在一些人們認為是很基本的營養常識上。一個很明顯的例子就是這些年來一直很受爭議的「低碳水化合物」飲食法。

這裡我想提供一些想法，讓父母了解飲食習慣會如何影響一個孩子的學習。

一位我常在報章雜誌上讀到的醫生/營養師認為：「我個人臨床的經驗顯示，產生記憶問題的個案似乎都和omega-3脂肪攝取的缺乏有很大的關係。」而到目前為止，最好的omega-3脂肪都是在魚肉中發現的。魚肉中的omega-3含有人類維持身體健康兩種很重要的酸類，DHA和EPA。這種兩種酸類在減低心臟病、癌症和其他疾病的發生上扮演很重要的角色。人腦很依賴DHA；研究中發現腦內DHA的指數過低和憂鬱症、精神分裂症、記

Yet another study observed, "During sleep deprivation there is 7 to 8 percent less blood flow to the brain that may impair your judgment and your storing of memories. It could also cause paranoia, depression, impair your immune function and possibly hormonal changes leading to obesity as well."

So as a rule, our children go to bed around 9 or 9:30 at night. Then when we wake up at 6:40 for 20 - 30 minutes of English before school, they have had 9 or 10 hours of sleep and they're alert and ready. Additionally, in that way, I can guarantee that they're getting the necessary daily English practice.

Nutrition

First, I wish to immediately state I am not a nutritionist. I can only say that I have been actively interested in nutrition for many years (I became more serious at university when I enrolled in a course on nutrition) and have actively exercised most of my life. On the other hand, if you regularly read reports regarding diet, you will find that professional nutritionists and researchers in the field often disagree with each other, even regarding what might be considered basic aspects of nutrition. A clear example is the debate that has been going for many years over the "low-carb" diets.

What I wish to offer here are simply some ideas that may help parents become aware how diet may affect a student's learning.

One doctor/nutritionist I often read believes that "a lack of omega-3 fats in the diet seems to be a strong indication in my clinical experience of those who struggle with memory problems." By far, the best type of omega-3 fats is found in fish. The omega-3 in fish is high in two fatty acids crucial to human health, DHA and EPA. These two fatty acids are pivotal in preventing heart disease, cancer, and many other diseases. The human brain is also highly dependent on DHA - low DHA levels have been linked to depression, schizophrenia, memory

憶喪失及老人癡呆症的發生有很大的關連。按時的服用魚油（像市面上找得到的魚肝油）是一個被認為用來增加omega-3攝取量的好方法，而能進一步改善一個人的健康情形。魚油含有豐富的高品質omega-3脂肪－－也就是含有EPA及DHA這些酸類－－而也因為他們的高純度，吃魚油不會像吃新鮮魚類時可能攝取到汞。

我在1987年來到亞洲，我看到亞洲的小孩子這幾年有一點很顯著的改變。我認為這是一個父母都應該要警惕的重大問題，可是這個問題卻很少有人關心；這個問題就是兒童肥胖症。當我剛來到亞洲時很少見到肥胖的小孩，但現在卻是隨處可見。

過重的小孩通常面臨較多的健康問題，包括（但不只有這些）第二類糖尿病心臟病、高膽固醇、高血壓、腸胃及骨骼問題，同時他們也比較容易因為自己的體重而產生自信心低落和憂鬱症。

除此之外，過重的青少年比其他人高出百分之七十的機率會成為過重的成人。這種延續性的肥胖，會比成年時才變胖帶來更多的健康問題。

造成兒童肥胖的原因有哪些？

一、 缺乏運動（看電視和打電動玩具；很少在戶外活動）

二、 喝汽水、果汁而不喝水

三、 吃糖果和過度加工的穀物食品（如麵包）

父母的忽視和否認會讓這個問題更加嚴重。一項研究顯示，所有嚴重過胖小孩的父母當中，只有三分之一認為他們的孩子是過胖的，而有百分之八的父母認為他們的孩子還不到肥胖的程度。

幸運的是，不管是大人或小孩子的肥胖都是可以被回復的，而這也的確是一種愛的表現。藉由鼓勵孩子適當的飲食和運動，父母可以免去他們很多不必要的痛苦。

loss, and a higher risk of developing Alzheimer's. Routine consumption of fish oil (like in pills) is a recommended method of increasing your omega-3 intake and improving your health. Fish oil contains high levels of the best omega-3 fats - those with the EPA and DHA fatty acids - and, as it is in pure form, does not pose the mercury risk of fresh fish.

I came to Asia in 1987 and there has been one very obvious and noticeable change in children. It is a major health problem I think parents should be alarmed about, but which seems to have received only minimal attention. What I'm talking about is childhood obesity. When I came to Asia, there were very few fat kids; now, they're everywhere!

Overweight and obese children are not only faced with increased health problems, including (but not limited to) type 2 diabetes, heart disease, high cholesterol, high blood pressure, gastrointestinal and orthopaedic problems, but they are also more likely to suffer from low self-esteem and depression as a result of their weight.

In addition, overweight adolescents have a 70 percent chance of becoming overweight or obese adults, which will then carry on to an even greater likelihood of developing serious health problems than if the obesity developed in adulthood.

What are the major causes of childhood obesity?

A. Lack of exercise (watching television and playing video games rather than playing outside)

B. Drinking soda and juice instead of water

C. Eating sugar and highly processed grains (like bread products)

Adding to the problem is parental ignorance or denial. According to one survey, only three percent of parents of severely obese children considered their child overweight, and eight percent of the parents actually considered them to be

第一步就是要你的孩子喝水；這可以大幅的減少他們從汽水和果汁中攝取到糖份的機會。看看以下這份報告：

含糖飲料=過重的小孩。2003年7月1日－－喝很多汽水和果汁的小孩不只是變胖，他們同時也犧牲掉了許多寶貴的營養。一項最新的研究發現，過多的含糖飲料是孩童過胖的主因，而也讓這些小孩在未來面臨更多潛在的健康問題。這項研究發現，如果小孩一天喝超過12盎司（也就是340c.c.）如汽水、果汁、罐裝飲料、或是由調味粉所製成的這些含糖飲料時，他們會比一天喝少於6盎司（也就是170c.c.）的小孩明顯變胖許多。

研究人員表示，喝汽水和果汁的小孩，同時也會喝較少的牛奶，因而減少了蛋白質和維他命的攝取。

如果孩童可以選擇，他們都會選含糖的飲料。研究人員表示，喜歡喝含糖飲料的小孩雖然得到了含糖飲料和果汁的高熱量，但他們並不會因此減少其他食物的攝取量，也因而攝取了過多的卡洛里而變胖。

先前的研究已經發現，飲用過多的含糖飲料對營養吸收有不良的影響，並會造成兒童肥胖；而這一次的研究則是第一次更長時間的觀察，孩童所吃的食物和飲料攝取量間的關係。

underweight!

Fortunately, obesity in both children and adults can be reversed, and this is truly and act of love. We can save our children needless suffering by encouraging them to eat an exercise properly.

The first step is to have your children drink water. This will drastically cut down on the amount of sugar your child consumes from soft drinks and fruit juices. Look at the surprising information in the following report.

Sugary drinks = fat kids July 1, 2003 -- Children who drink a lot of soft drinks and fruit juice may not only gain weight, but they may also be sacrificing valuable nutrition. A new study shows too many sugary drinks may be fueling the increase in childhood obesity and putting children at risk for health problems in the future. The study showed that children who drank more than 12 ounces (340 grams) of sweetened drinks, such as soft drinks, fruit juice, bottled tea, or drinks made from flavored powders, gained significantly more weight than those who drank less than 6 ounces (170 grams) of the sweet stuff per day.

Researchers say children who drank sugary soft drinks and fruit juice also drank less milk and missed out on protein and vitamins.

When given a choice, the children chose sugary drinks. Despite the high calorie content of sweetened soft drinks and fruit juices, researchers say children who drank sugary drinks did not reduce the quantity or calorie content of the foods they ate, so their daily calorie intake rose and they gained

接下來，讓你的孩子吃健康、營養的食物，而不要吃大多數超級市場販賣的過度加工食品。這也代表著減少加工過穀類和糖類的攝取，因為這是大多數人胖肥的主要原因。另一個胖肥的主因是「速食」。在美國，有將近三分之一年齡介於４到１９歲的孩童每天都吃速食，這讓每一個孩童一年約增加了六磅，也因而增加了肥胖的危機。當我們發現速食業者一年花費在擴展兒童市場的金額高達數十億元時，以上所提到的數字似乎也就不足為奇了。觀察一下電視黃金時段的廣告，你會發現許多速食業者針對兒童族群所做的促銷廣告。從1970年開始計算的話，現代小孩食用速食的量已經增加了5倍之多。

要求小孩放棄這些垃圾食物的過程可能不是那麼容易，但小孩的飲食習慣其實都是從他們生活周遭的人所學來的。所以，父母本身有均衡的飲食和運動習慣也就相當重要了。

運動是另外一個很重要的因素。過重或是肥胖的小孩每天至少需運動30分鐘以上。任何能讓你的小孩遠離電視的活動都是好的，剛開始可以先和你的小孩一起散步，之後再逐漸增加運動的強度，開始從事如騎腳踏車、慢跑、打籃球或足球這一類的運動。

在過去，大多數人的知道服用維他命雖不會有立即的效果，但長期下來對身體健康會有好處。最近，研究人員分析超過125種的醫學和科學研究報告，並提出具體的證據來證明綜合維他命的好處，以及服用綜合維他命所能節省的醫療資源。研究人員表示，按時服用綜合維他命可以降低心臟動脈方

weight.

Previous studies have found excessive sweetened drink consumption adversely affects nutrition and promotes childhood obesity, but it's the first study to monitor children's food and drink consumption for an extended period of time.

Next, have your child eat a healthy diet of whole, nutritious foods rather than the processed ones that line most grocery store shelves. This includes cutting out processed grains and sugar, as these are two of the major culprits behind weight gain. Another major culprit is fast food. Close to one-third of U.S. children aged 4 to 19 eat fast food daily, which likely adds about six extra pounds per child per year and increases the risk of obesity. This is not surprising considering that fast-food companies spend billions of dollars each year on marketing aimed at kids. Watch a few hours of prime-time TV and count how many fast food commercials are aimed at kids. The amount of fast food that children consume has increased fivefold since 1970.

Children may have a hard time giving up their junk food snacks. Your children will learn their eating habits from those around them, so it's important that parents are also eating well and exercising.

Exercise is another extremely important factor. Overweight and obese children will need at least 30 minutes of exercise a day. Any activity that gets your child up and away from the television set is a good idea. At first you can try walking with your child, and then gradually increase the intensity to include activities such as biking, jogging and active sports like basketball or

面的疾病，並增加人體免疫系統的功能！

對我而言，我把每天服用綜合維他命視為是理所當然的事；這既不用花什麼錢，也不會有什麼傷害，而且有越來越多的證據顯示，長期服用綜合維他命對一個人的健康有很正面的影響！

運動

在電動機具被發明以前，得到適當的運動量是很容易的，因為當時的人不論到哪裡都必須走路或騎腳踏車。今天，人們必須花更多的心力才能維持身材在正常範圍內。我深信適當的運動不但可以幫助我們維持身心健康，還能讓我們可以整天有更好的專注力，這對需要花很多時間讀書的學生而言正是最重要的。舉例來說，我在讀國、高中和大學時，不論我有多忙，我都還是找時間做適當的運動，而我也相信這個習慣和我優異的學習成績表現有很大的相關。除了我自身的經驗之外，以下這個最近的研究結果也可以佐證我的說法。

football/soccer.

In the past, taking a daily multivitamin has largely been an act of faith. Recently, researchers analyzed more than 125 clinical studies and additional scientific literature to determine the health benefits of multivitamins, and the subsequent savings in healthcare bills. Researchers said that regular multivitamin use demonstrated protection from the risk of coronary artery disease, as well as benefits to the immune system.

For me, taking a good multivitamin is a no-brainer. It's inexpensive, it can't do any harm, and the evidence is mounting that long-term multivitamin use may provide a host of positive health benefits.

Exercise

Before the advent of motorized vehicles, obtaining adequate levels of exercise was quite easy, since we had to walk or ride bicycles everywhere. Today, we have to go to a little more effort to stay fit. I strongly believe that a moderate level of exercise both helps in maintaining good health and improves our mental abilities, thereby allowing us to focus better all day long, which is critical for students who need to study for long periods. For example, during my student years in junior high, high school and four years at university, I tried to make sure I exercised regularly, no matter how busy I was, and I believe that helped me achieve high marks throughout. Beyond my personal testimony, I can offer the following recent research：

2003年10月17日(CNN)報導：最近一項研究顯示規律的運動習慣可以減緩記憶喪失的速度，且根據一本新書的記戴，一個人某方面的記憶也會因運動的習慣而逐年改善。

根據紐約醫學院Antonio Convit博士的說法，人們用來加強身體健康的運動同時也對腦部有正面的影響。

伊利諾大學Urbana分校的研究員Stan Colcombe表示，「長時間的從事心肺運動可以減少隨年紀增加而失去的組織數量」。

這其中包括了腦部組織，而減少腦部組織的喪失也就代表著一個人可以記得更多美好的回憶。

Colcombe是伊利諾大學研究小組中的一位成員，這個小組分析一批年紀超過55歲者的腦部斷層掃描，他們發現這些人的腦部構造有很大的不同。身體狀況良好的人腦部的灰質構造較好。

減重同時也可以改善一個人的記憶力。「減重」可以改善身體管理葡萄糖的功能，而我們發現，有效的管理葡萄糖和良好的記憶力有很大的關聯。

血糖的不當管理不但會影響一個人記憶的能力，同時也會影響腦部某些部份的組織大小。Convit發現，一個無法有效管理葡萄糖的身體會造成一個人腦部海馬組織的縮小，而這部份腦部組織正是和記根據伊利諾大學Urbana分校的研究，適當的心肺運動，如每周幾次的快走，身體所得到的活動量其實也就夠了。

October 17, 2003 (CNN) Recent studies indicate that a simple exercise routine helps put the brakes on memory loss. And one aspect of memory automatically improves with age, according to a new book.

What you do to improve your physical health may actually go to your head, according to Dr. Antonio Convit of the New York University School of Medicine.

"Cardiovascular exercise that's done over a longer period of time will tend to reduce the amount of tissue you lose as you age," says Stan Colcombe, a researcher at the University of Illinois-Urbana.

That includes brain tissue, and losing less of it may mean keeping more precious memories.

Colcombe was part of a team of researchers at the University of Illinois who looked at MRI scans of people 55 or older and discovered dramatic differences in their brains. The people who were physically fit had gray matter in better shape.

Losing weight can also improve memory function. "[Losing weight] will improve how you regulate your glucose, and we have shown that improved glucose regulation is associated with better memory."

Dealing with blood sugar poorly not only affects one's ability to remember but also the size of one area of the brain. Convit found that individuals with poor glucose regulation had a smaller hippocampus, the part of the brain dealing with memory.

我們很快的來複習以上所講到的要點：

* 良好的睡眠
* 均衡的營養
* 避免肥胖
* 運動

身為父母，我們可以幫助我們的孩子得到健康，並達成終身學習的目的。這是我們的責任。

最後一點

最後讓我以感謝你來做結，感謝你讀這一本書。我們禱告這一本書除了可以讓你成為一個更稱職的父母外，在幫忙孩子學好英文的過程中，希望這一本書也可以讓你在時間和金錢上的投資做最好的決定。在外面有許多很好的老師和課程，而有些事則是你可以做以幫助您的孩子學好英文的。

我們獻上最誠摯的祝福，希望您的小孩可以學好這個美麗的語言，也希望藉著這個語言，您的小孩可以探索這個愈來愈小，但卻也愈來愈複雜的世界，並為他們自己創造出無限美好的機會！

Moderate cardiovascular exercise, such as a brisk 30-minute walk a few times a week, should do the trick, according to the University of Illinois-Urbana study.

Let's quickly summarize the above main points:

* Adequate sleep
* Proper nutrition
* Avoid obesity
* Exercise

As parents, we can help our children obtain good health and become better students for life. It is our responsibility.

Final Note

Let us close by first thanking you. Thank you for reading this book. We do pray it will benefit you in your quest to be a good parent and to help your child learn English well, and that it will assist you in making the wisest investment of your time and money. There are excellent teachers and programs out there, and there are specific things you can do to help your child learn English well.

We send our blessings to you and wish you and your child the best in mastering this wonderful language to successfully navigate in this increasingly small and complex world, and be able to take full advantage of all the wonderful opportunities that are out there.

英語資優生--如何挑選英文家教與補習班

作　　者：安德魯、陳俊郎
出 版 者：葉子出版股份有限公司
發 行 人：宋宏智
企劃主編：林淑雯
媒體企劃：汪君瑜
責任編輯：陳裕升
美術編輯：小豬
封面設計：小豬
印　　務：許鈞棋
專案行銷：張曜鐘、林欣穎、吳惠娟
地　　址：台北市新生南路三段88號5樓之6
電　　話：（02）23660309　傳真：（02）23660310
E-mail ：service@ycrc.com.tw
網　　址：http://www.ycrc.com.tw
郵撥帳號：19735365　戶名：葉忠賢
印　　刷：上海印刷廠股份有限公司
法律顧問：北辰著作權事務所
初版一刷：2005年2月　定價：新台幣 220 元
I S B N ：986-7609-55-7

國家圖書館出版品預行編目資料

英語資優生：如何挑選英文家教與補習班 /
安德魯, 陳俊郎作. -- 初版.
-- 臺北市：葉子, 2005 [民94] 面 ； 公分.
-- (向日葵) ISBN 986-7609-55-7 (平裝)
1. 英國語言 - 學習方法
805.1　94001458

總 經 銷： 揚智文化事業股份有限公司
地　　址： 台北市新生南路三段88號5樓之6
電　　話： （02）23660309
傳　　真： （02）23660310

廣 告 回 信
臺灣北區郵政管理局登記證
北 台 字 第 8719 號
免 貼 郵 票

106-□□
台北市新生南路3段88號5樓之6

揚智文化事業股份有限公司 收

□□□-□□
地址： 市縣 鄉鎮市區 路街 段 巷 弄 號 樓
姓名：

書號 L8201 書名 英語資優生--如何挑選英文家教與補習班

葉子出版股份有限公司

讀・者・回・函

感謝您購買本公司出版的書籍。
爲了更接近讀者的想法，出版您想閱讀的書籍，在此需要勞駕您詳細爲我們填寫回函，您的一份心力，將使我們更加努力！！

1.姓名：＿＿＿＿＿＿
2.性別：□男 □女
3.生日／年齡：西元＿＿＿年＿＿＿月＿＿＿日＿＿歲
4.教育程度：□高中職以下 □專科及大學 □碩士 □博士以上
5.職業別：□學生□服務業□軍警□公教□資訊□傳播□金融□貿易
□製造生產□家管□其他＿＿＿＿＿
6.購書方式／地點名稱：□書店＿＿＿□量販店＿＿＿□網路＿＿＿□郵購＿＿＿
□書展＿＿＿□其他＿＿
7.如何得知此出版訊息：□媒體＿＿＿□書訊＿＿＿□書店＿＿＿□其他＿＿＿
8.購買原因：□喜歡作者□對書籍內容感興趣□生活或工作需要□其他
9.書籍編排：□專業水準□賞心悅目□設計普通□有待加強
10.書籍封面：□非常出色□平凡普通□毫不起眼
11. E－mail：＿＿＿＿＿＿＿＿＿＿＿＿＿＿＿＿＿＿＿＿
12喜歡哪一類型的書籍：＿＿＿＿＿＿＿＿＿＿＿＿＿＿＿＿
13.月收入：□兩萬到三萬□三到四萬□四到五萬□五萬以上□十萬以上
14.您認為本書定價：□過高□適當□便宜
15.希望本公司出版哪方面的書籍：＿＿＿＿＿＿＿＿＿＿＿＿
16.本公司企劃的書籍分類裡，有哪些書系是您感到興趣的？
□忘憂草（身心靈）□愛麗絲（流行時尚）□紫薇（愛情）□三色董（財經）
□ 銀杏（飲食保健）□風信子（旅遊文學）□向日葵（青少年）
17.您的寶貴意見：

＿＿＿＿＿＿＿＿＿＿＿＿＿＿＿＿＿＿＿＿＿＿＿＿＿＿＿＿

☆填寫完畢後，可直接寄回（免貼郵票）。
我們將不定期寄發新書資訊，並優先通知您
其他優惠活動，再次感謝您！！

根

以讀者爲其根本

莖

用生活來做支撐

葉

引發思考或功用

獲取效益或趣味